The entire pack of men rushed Tarzan from all sides with knives, chairs and fists. The man with the club swung it with enough power to crush Tarzan's head.

But the brain, agility and muscles that had been a match for the mighty strength and cruel craftiness of Terkoz, the great ape, and Numa, the lion, were not to be easy prey for Parisian thugs. Tarzan charged the man with the club, dodged its swing, and felled him in his tracks with a terrific blow on the chin. Then he turned to the others. This was great sport: the joy of battle, the lust of blood. He shed civilization as a snake sheds its skin. The ten burly crooks found themselves penned up in a small room with a wild beast, against whose muscles their own were puny.

A Background Note about the Book

The Return of Tarzan begins in about 1909, with Tarzan aboard an ocean liner sailing from the United States to France. If you haven't read *Tarzan of the Apes*, the book that precedes this one, you may be surprised to find the legendary jungle hero sipping cocktails and mingling with the French nobility. A little background may be helpful:

In *Tarzan of the Apes*, we learned how Tarzan's parents were stranded and died on the coast of Africa. Their infant son was adopted by a tribe of great apes. Knowing nothing of his true identity as heir to the title Lord Greystoke, Tarzan grew into the strong and sometimes savage "king of the jungle." But Tarzan then encounters the beautiful Jane Porter and William Cecil Clayton, Tarzan's own cousin and the supposed heir to the Greystoke fortune. Tarzan saves Jane's life and falls in love with her, but believes she loves Cecil. At the end of *Tarzan of the Apes*, Tarzan has followed Jane to Wisconsin. He learns his true identity and his right to the Greystoke fortune, but nobly keeps the secret to himself in order that Cecil and Jane might enjoy the Greystoke money and title. The reader suspects that Jane is secretly in love with Tarzan, but that question is still unanswered as *The Return of Tarzan* begins.

Another question that might be on your mind: if Tarzan was raised by apes, how does he know how to communicate with human beings? As a child, Tarzan discovered his dead parents' deserted cabin. There he found books with which he taught himself to read and understand English, even though he could not speak it. When he met Jane and her group, he communicated with them through notes. One of them, a Frenchman named D'Arnot who becomes Tarzan's friend, taught him to speak French. And so at the beginning of *The Return of Tarzan*, our jungle king is traveling as a French-speaking African named "Jean Tarzan."

EDGAR RICE BURROUGHS

THE RETURN OF TARZAN

Edited, with an Afterword,
by Jonathan Kelley

TP THE TOWNSEND LIBRARY

THE RETURN OF TARZAN

TP **THE TOWNSEND LIBRARY**

For more titles in the Townsend Library,
visit our website: **www.townsendpress.com**

All new material in this edition is
copyright © 2004 by Townsend Press.
Printed in the United States of America

0 9 8 7 6 5 4 3 2 1

Townsend Press, Inc.
1038 Industrial Drive
West Berlin, New Jersey 08091

ISBN 1-59194-020-6

Library of Congress Control Number:
2003112999

TABLE OF CONTENTS

CHAPTER 1

The Affair on the Ocean Liner

"*Magnifique!*" exclaimed the Countess de Coude under her breath to her husband, who was absorbed in a book.

"Eh? What is so magnificent?" questioned the Count, glancing over to her.

"Oh, nothing at all, my dear," replied the Countess, blushing slightly. "I was but recalling with admiration those stupendous 'skyscrapers' of New York." Her husband found that odd; he remembered that when she had first gazed at the New York skyline, she called the tall buildings 'horrid.' The Countess settled back in her chair and resumed reading a magazine.

Presently the Count put down his book. "This is tiresome, Olga. I think that I shall see if anyone wants to play cards."

"You are not very gallant, my husband," replied the young woman, smiling, "but as I am equally bored, I can forgive you. Go and play at your tiresome old cards, then, if you will."

When he had gone, she let her eyes wander slyly to the figure of a tall young man stretched lazily in a nearby chair.

"Magnifique!" she breathed once more.

The Countess Olga de Coude was twenty, her husband forty. While she was a very loyal wife, the marriage had been arranged by her father. She was not passionately in love, and while her thoughts remained faithful, this young man was still nice to look at.

As she furtively watched him, he rose to leave the deck. The Countess de Coude called to a passing steward. "Who is that gentleman?" she asked.

"He is booked, Madame, as Monsieur Tarzan, of Africa," replied the steward.

"Rather a large estate," she thought, with greater interest.

Tarzan walked slowly toward the smoking-room, and observed two men whispering excitedly just outside. He would have ignored them, except that one sent a guilty look in his direction. Both had dark hair and evil expressions, reminding him of the villains he had seen in plays in Paris. He entered the smoking-room, sat down by himself, and ordered a cocktail. He was in no mood for conversation, and let his mind run sorrowfully over the past few weeks.

He had often wondered about his decision to renounce his birthright. While he liked William Cecil Clayton, Lord Greystoke, it was not for

Clayton's sake that Tarzan had given up his rightful heritage. He owed Clayton nothing. He gave it up for Jane, the woman both men loved, and whom a twist of fate had given to Clayton. Tarzan was devoted to her happiness, and he had learned about civilized persons: they greatly valued money and position and could not tolerate life without them. To take these from Clayton would also have taken them from Jane.

Tarzan could do nothing that would plunge Jane Porter, born to both money and position, into hardship. The notion that she might desert Clayton if he lost his title and estates never crossed his mind, for he credited others with his own brand of simple loyalty—and in Jane's case at least, he was right. She would have remained by her husband's side through any such misfortune.

Tarzan's thoughts drifted to the future. He tried to look forward to his return to the cruel, fierce jungle where he had spent twenty of his twenty-two years. But who would welcome his return? No one. Only Tantor, the elephant, could he call his friend. The others would hunt him or flee from him, as before; not even the apes of his own tribe would befriend him. Civilization had changed him, taught him to want companionship. A world without friends—with no one to talk to—would be joyless.

As he sat thinking, he happened to glance into a mirror on the wall and saw four men playing cards at a table behind him. One left, and then another approached, courteously offering to fill the vacant chair so that the game might continue. Tarzan was interested, for the newcomer was the smaller of the two he had seen skulking just outside the smoking-room. The ape-man examined the players, but he knew the name of only one: Count Raoul de Coude, whom an over-attentive steward had pointed out as a high official in the French Ministry of War.

Now the other swarthy plotter had entered, and was standing behind de Coude's chair. All Tarzan's attention was on him. The man looked furtively about, but did not notice Tarzan's reflected scrutiny. He took something out of his pocket, palming it. Slowly the hand approached the Count, and then deftly transferred it into the Count's pocket. The man remained standing where he could watch the Frenchman's cards, closely watched by Tarzan.

The game went on for some ten more minutes, until the Count won a considerable wager from the conspirator. Then Tarzan saw the fellow behind the Count's chair nod to his accomplice, who instantly arose and pointed a finger at the nobleman.

"Had I known that Monsieur was a professional card shark, I would not have joined the game," he said.

Instantly the Count and the two other players were on their feet. De Coude's face went white.

"What do you mean, sir?" he cried. "Do you know to whom you speak?"

"I speak to one who cheats at cards," replied the fellow.

De Coude leaned across the table and slapped the man full in the mouth. The others separated them. "There is some mistake, sir," cried one. "Why, this is Count de Coude, of France. He would not cheat."

"If I am mistaken," said the accuser, "I shall gladly apologize. But first let Monsieur le Count explain the extra cards which I saw him drop into his side pocket."

Then the man whom Tarzan had seen plant those cards turned to sneak from the room. To his annoyance, he found the exit barred by a tall, gray-eyed stranger.

"Pardon," said the man roughly, attempting to pass to one side.

"Wait," said Tarzan.

"But why, Monsieur?" exclaimed the other petulantly. "Let me pass."

"Wait," said Tarzan. "I think that you may be able to explain something here."

The fellow now lost his temper, cursed Tarzan, and tried to push him to one side. The ape-man smiled as he twisted the big fellow about, grasped him by his coat collar and escorted him back to the table, struggling and swearing in futile complaint. It was Nikolai Rokoff's first experience with the muscles that had brought down Numa, the lion, and Terkoz, the great bull ape.

The other card players stood looking expectantly at the Count. Several other passengers were now watching to see the outcome.

"The fellow is crazy," said de Coude. "Gentlemen, I implore that one of you search me."

"The accusation is ridiculous," said one of the players.

"You have but to inspect Monsieur's coat pocket and you will see that the accusation is quite serious," insisted the accuser. And then, as the others still hesitated: "Come, I shall do it myself if no one else will," and he stepped forward.

"No, Monsieur," said de Coude. "I will submit to a search only at the hands of a gentleman."

"It is unnecessary to search the Count," said a tall onlooker. "The cards are in his pocket. I myself saw them placed there."

They all turned in surprise. They saw a very well-built young man urging a resisting captive toward them by the scruff of his neck.

"It is a conspiracy," cried de Coude angrily. "There are no cards in my coat," and with that he ran his hand into his pocket. As he did so, tense silence settled over the little group.

The French nobleman went dead white, and then very slowly he withdrew his hand, and in it were three cards. He looked at them in horrified surprise. Expressions of pity and contempt tinged the features of those who were watching the death of a man's honor.

"It is a conspiracy, Monsieur." It was the gray-eyed stranger who spoke. "Gentlemen," he continued, "the cards were placed there without Monsieur le Count's knowledge as he sat at play. I saw it all in the mirror; this person, who I intercepted in the act of escaping, placed the cards in Monsieur's pocket."

De Coude glanced from Tarzan to the evil-looking man in his grasp.

"*Mon dieu*, Nikolai!" he cried. "You?"

Then the Count turned to the man who had accused him of cheating, and eyed him intently for a moment. "And you, Monsieur. I did not recognize you without your beard. It quite disguises you, Paulvitch. It is quite clear, gentlemen."

"What shall we do with them, Monsieur?" asked Tarzan. "Turn them over to the captain?"

"No, my friend," said the Count hastily. "It is a personal matter, and I beg that you will let it drop. It is enough that I am proven innocent, and the less we have to do with these fellows, the better. But, Monsieur, how can I thank you for the great kindness you have done me? Please accept my card, and if ever I may serve you, I am yours to command."

Tarzan released Rokoff, who made a hasty exit with his confederate Paulvitch. Just as he was leaving, Rokoff turned to Tarzan and spoke in a low voice. "Monsieur will regret his interference."

Tarzan smiled. Bowing to de Coude, he handed

him his own card.

The Count read:

M. JEAN C. TARZAN

"Monsieur Tarzan may indeed wish that he had never befriended me," said the count, "for I can assure him that he has made enemies of two of the worst scoundrels in all Europe. Avoid them, Monsieur, by all means."

"I have had more awe-inspiring enemies, my dear Count," replied Tarzan with a quiet smile, "yet I am still alive and unworried. I doubt they can harm me."

"Let us hope not, Monsieur," said de Coude; "but be watchful. You have made at least one unforgiving enemy today. To call Nikolai Rokoff a devil would be to insult Satan."

That night as Tarzan entered his cabin he found a folded note that had been pushed beneath the door. He opened it and read:

M. TARZAN:

Doubtless you did not realize the seriousness of your offense, or you would not have done as you did today. I am willing to believe that you acted in ignorance. For this reason I shall gladly permit you to offer an apology, and on receiving your promise not to again interfere in affairs that do not concern you, I shall drop the matter.

Otherwise . . . but I am sure that you will see the wisdom of adopting the course I suggest.

Very respectfully,
NIKOLAI ROKOFF

Tarzan permitted himself a moment's grim smile, then promptly forgot about the matter and went to bed.

In a nearby cabin, the Countess de Coude was speaking to her husband. "Why so grave, my dear Raoul?" she asked. "You have been so glum all evening. What worries you?"

"Olga, Nikolai Rokoff is on board. Did you know it?"

"Nikolai!" she exclaimed. "But it cannot be, Raoul. Nikolai is under arrest in Germany."

"So I thought myself until I saw him today with that other arch-scoundrel, Paulvitch. Olga, I cannot endure his persecution much longer—not even for you. Sooner or later I shall turn him over to the authorities. I am half minded to explain the situation to the captain before we land. On a French liner it would be an easy matter, Olga, to permanently end this problem of ours," he finished grimly.

"Oh, no, Raoul!" cried the Countess, sinking to her knees before him as he sat on the sofa. "Remember your promise to me. Tell me, Raoul, that you will not do that. Do not even threaten him, Raoul."

De Coude took his wife's hands in his and gazed on her troubled face for some time before he spoke.

"As you wish, Olga," he said at length. "I cannot understand. He has forfeited all claim to your love, loyalty, or respect. He is a menace to your life and honor, and that of your husband. I hope you will never regret this defense of him."

"I do not defend him, Raoul," she interrupted vehemently. "I hate him as much as you do, but—oh, Raoul, blood is thicker than water."

"I would today have liked to see his blood," growled de Coude grimly. "They conspired to stain my honor, Olga."

He told her all that had happened. "Had it not been for this utter stranger, they would have succeeded, for who would have accepted my unsupported word against the damning evidence of those hidden cards? I had almost begun to doubt myself when this Monsieur Tarzan dragged your precious Nikolai before us, and explained the whole cowardly transaction."

"Monsieur Tarzan?" asked the Countess, in evident surprise.

"Yes. Do you know him, Olga?"

"I have seen him. A steward pointed him out to me."

"I did not know that he was a celebrity," said the Count.

Olga de Coude changed the subject. She might find it difficult to explain just why the steward had pointed out the handsome Monsieur Tarzan to her. Perhaps her husband read it in her face, for his expression seemed curious. "Ah," she thought to herself, "a guilty conscience is a very suspicious thing."

CHAPTER 2

Forging Bonds of Hate and —?

Late the following afternoon, Tarzan again came unexpectedly upon Rokoff and Paulvitch, and again just when they least welcomed his company.

They were standing in a quiet spot on deck when Tarzan first saw them. Their backs were to him and they were arguing heatedly with a young, well-dressed woman. She was too heavily veiled for him to see her features, but she seemed frightened. The conversation was in a strange language; from the tones, the woman seemed to be pleading, and Rokoff's voice sounded threatening. After a short time, the ape-man sensed that Rokoff was about to harm her; he eased closer. Sure enough, Rokoff next seized the woman roughly by the wrist, twisting it as if to wring a promise from her through pain.

We cannot know what Rokoff meant to do next, for it never happened. Steel fingers gripped his shoulder and swung him roughly around to meet the cold gray eyes of the same stranger who had foiled him the day before.

"Saints!" screamed the infuriated Rokoff. "What do you mean? Again you dare insult Nikolai Rokoff?"

"This is my answer to your note, Monsieur," said Tarzan, hurling the Russian violently away and sending him sprawling into the rail.

"Son of a dog!" shrieked Rokoff. "Pig! You shall die for this!" Springing to his feet, he rushed upon Tarzan, reaching to draw a revolver from his hip pocket. The girl shrank back in terror.

"Nikolai!" she cried. "Do not—oh, do not do that! Quick, Monsieur, run, or he will surely kill you!"

Tarzan instead advanced to meet Rokoff. "Do not make a fool of yourself, Monsieur," he said.

Rokoff, enraged at his humiliation, had at last managed to draw the revolver. He stopped, leveled it at Tarzan's heart and pulled the trigger. The hammer fell with a futile click on an empty chamber, and the ape-man's hand shot out like the head of an angry snake. There was a quick wrench, and the revolver sailed far out across the ship's rail into the Atlantic.

For a moment the two men stood facing one another. Rokoff regained his self-control, and now spoke first.

"Twice now, Monsieur has seen fit to interfere in matters which do not concern him. Twice he has chosen to humiliate Nikolai Rokoff. The first offense was overlooked on the assumption that

Monsieur acted in ignorance, but this one shall not be. If Monsieur does not know who Nikolai Rokoff is, he soon shall."

"Monsieur knows that Nikolai Rokoff is a coward and a scoundrel," replied Tarzan scornfully, "and that is all Monsieur cares or needs to know of him." He turned to ask the woman if the man had hurt her, but she had disappeared. Then, without even a glance toward Rokoff and his companion, he continued his stroll along the deck.

What manner of conspiracy was afoot, wondered Tarzan. There was something familiar about the veiled woman's appearance, but he could not be sure he had ever seen her before. He had noticed a peculiar ring on the hand that Rokoff had twisted. He would watch for it, in hopes of learning her identity and seeing whether Rokoff annoyed her any further.

Tarzan went to his deck chair, and sat thinking about all the instances of human cruelty, selfishness, and spite he had witnessed in the past four years. It had been that long since his first sight of another human being: the lean, black African warrior Kulonga, whose poisoned arrow had slain Kala, the great she-ape, and robbed young Tarzan of the only mother he had ever known. He recalled the mutineers' murder of their own comrades; the abandonment of Professor Porter and his party by the mutineers; the cruelty of the tribe of Mbonga to their captives; the petty jealousies of the civil and military officers of the West African colony that had been his first introduction to civilization.

"Mon dieu!" he thought, "but they are all alike. Cheating, murdering, lying, fighting—all for money to purchase the soft pleasures of weaklings. Always bound by silly customs, slaves to their unhappy situation, while thinking of themselves as the lords of creation enjoying life's only true pleasures. No creature of the jungle would just stand by while another stole his mate. This is a silly world, and Tarzan of the Apes was a fool to renounce the freedom and the happiness of his jungle to join it."

Presently he got the feeling that he was being watched, and the old instincts of the jungle took over. Tarzan wheeled so quickly that the young woman did not even have time to avert her eyes before his gray eyes met them, and she blushed. He did not look away. She was quite attractive, and there was something familiar about her. He resumed his former position, and was aware that she had gotten up to leave the deck. He turned to watch her, hoping to satisfy his mild curiosity about her identity.

She raised her hand to the back of her neck as she left, and on a finger he saw the same ring that he had seen on the veiled woman's hand.

So this beautiful woman was the one Rokoff had been persecuting. Tarzan wondered who she might be, and what one so lovely could have to do with the surly, bearded Russian.

After dinner that evening, Tarzan strolled forward, chatted with the second officer awhile, then was left by himself watching the moonlight on the gently rolling waters. Half hidden by some equipment, the two men who approached along the deck did not see him, but he overheard them talking. The voices were those of Rokoff and Paulvitch, and what he heard proved that they were up to no good: "And if she screams you may choke her until—"

He trailed them to the smoking-room area, but they merely stopped there to check and see who was inside. They then headed directly to the first-class cabins on the promenade deck, Tarzan still following discreetly. As they halted before a polished hardwood door, Tarzan slipped into the shadows a dozen feet behind them.

To their knock, a woman's voice asked in French: "Who is it?"

"It is I, Olga—Nikolai," was the answer, in Rokoff's now familiar rough voice. "May I come in?"

"Why do you not leave me alone, Nikolai?" came the feminine voice from behind the thin panel. "I have never harmed you."

"Come, come, Olga," urged the man, in soothing tones. "I ask but a few words with you. I shall not harm you, nor even enter your cabin; but I cannot shout my message through the door."

Tarzan heard the catch click as it was released from the inside. He stepped out from his hiding place far enough to see what came next. Uppermost in his mind were the sinister words he had heard a few moments before out on the deck.

Rokoff was standing directly in front of the door, with Paulvitch flattened against the corridor wall nearby. The door opened. Rokoff half entered the room and stood with his back against the door, speaking in a low whisper to the woman, whom Tarzan could not see. Then Tarzan heard the woman's voice speak in French, just loud enough to overhear:

"No, Nikolai," she was saying, "it is useless. Threaten as you will, I shall never submit to your demands. Leave the room, please! You have no right to be here, and you promised not to enter."

"Very well, Olga, I shall not enter, but before I am done with you, you shall wish a thousand times that you had done immediately what I have asked. In the end I shall win anyway, so you might as well save me trouble and time, and prevent disgrace for yourself and your—"

"Never, Nikolai!" interrupted the woman. Then Tarzan saw Rokoff turn and nod to Paulvitch, who sprang quickly past Rokoff into the cabin. The door closed, leaving Rokoff outside. Tarzan heard the click of the lock as Paulvitch turned it from the inside. Rokoff remained standing at the door, head bent to catch the words of the two inside. A nasty smile curled his bearded lip.

Tarzan could hear the woman's raised voice, ordering the fellow to leave her cabin. "I shall send for my husband," she cried. "He will show you no mercy."

Paulvitch's sneering laugh came through the polished panels. "The purser will fetch your husband, Madame," said he. "In fact, that officer has already been notified that you are entertaining a man other than your husband behind the locked door of your cabin."

"Bah!" cried the woman. "My husband will know!"

"Most assuredly. But the purser will not, nor will the newspaper reporters who shall mysteriously hear of it when we land. They will think it a fine story, and so will all your friends when they read about it at breakfast on—let me see, this is Tuesday—yes, when they read about it at breakfast next Friday morning. They will all find it even more interesting that the man Madame entertained is a Russian servant—her brother's valet, to be quite exact."

"Alexei Paulvitch," came the woman's voice, cold and fearless, "you are a coward, and when I whisper a certain name in your ear you will reconsider your demands and your threats, and then you will leave my cabin quickly and never again annoy me." There came a moment's silence, in which Tarzan could imagine the woman leaning toward the scoundrel and whispering something into his ear. Only a moment of silence, and then a startled oath from the man—the scuffling of feet—a woman's scream—and silence.

The cry had barely ceased before the ape-man had leaped from his hiding-place. Rokoff started to run, but Tarzan dragged him back by the collar. Neither spoke. The ape-man threw his giant shoulder against the frail door panel, and in a shower of splinters he entered the cabin, dragging Rokoff after him.

Quickly scanning the room, he saw Paulvitch struggling with the woman on the couch with his fingers gripping her fair throat. His victim's hands beat futilely at his face, tearing desperately at the cruel fingers that were forcing the life from her.

The noise of the entrance brought Paulvitch to his feet, where he stood glowering menacingly at Tarzan. The girl sat up shakily on the couch, one hand on her bruised throat, her breath coming in little gasps. Although disheveled and very pale, Tarzan recognized her: the young woman he had caught staring at him on deck earlier in the day.

"What is the meaning of this?" said Tarzan, turning to Rokoff, who was clearly the chief plotter. The man remained silent, scowling. "Touch the button, please," said the ape-man to the woman; "we will have one of the ship's officers here. This affair has gone quite far enough."

"No, no," she cried, coming suddenly to her feet. "Please do not. I am sure that there was no real intention to harm me. I angered this person, and he lost control of himself, that is all. I would not care to have the matter go further, please, Monsieur," and there was such a pleading note in her voice that Tarzan could not press the matter, though his better judgment told him to go straight to the authorities.

"You wish me to do nothing, then?" he asked.

"Nothing, please," she replied.

"You are content that these two scoundrels should continue to harass you?"

She did not seem to know how to answer that, and looked very troubled. Tarzan saw a malicious grin of triumph curl Rokoff's lip. Evidently she was afraid to speak freely.

"Then," said Tarzan, "I shall act on my own responsibility. To you," he continued, turning to Rokoff, "and this other lout, I say that from now on to the end of the voyage I shall keep an eye on you. If I notice either of you again even remotely annoying this young woman, you will answer to me. I promise that you will not like what I do. Now get out of here." He grabbed Rokoff and Paulvitch each by the scruff of the neck and shoved them through the doorway, giving each some added encouragement with his boot. Then he turned back to the stateroom and the woman, who was looking at him in wide-eyed astonishment.

"And you, Madame, will do me a great favor if you will let me know if either of those rascals troubles you further."

"Ah, Monsieur," she answered, "I hope that you will not suffer for the kind deed you attempted. You have made a very wicked and resourceful enemy, who will stop at nothing to satisfy his hatred. You must be very careful indeed, Monsieur—"

"Pardon me, Madame, my name is Tarzan."

" . . . Monsieur Tarzan. And though I would not consent to notify the officers, I am sincerely grateful to you for your brave and chivalrous protection. Good night, Monsieur Tarzan. I shall never forget the debt I owe you," and, with a sweet smile that displayed a row of perfect teeth, she curtsied to him. He wished her good night, and made his way on deck.

Tarzan was quite puzzled. This Rokoff character and his accomplice were abusing both this woman and the Count de Coude. Yet, strangely, neither would allow them to be brought to justice. Before he went to sleep he thought many times about the beautiful young woman whom the tangled web of fate had introduced to him. He did not even know her name, but to judge by the gold band on her left hand, she was married to some lucky man.

Most of the rest of the voyage passed without Tarzan seeing anything further of the actors in this little drama. Late in the afternoon on the last day, he chanced to meet the young woman on deck. She smiled pleasantly at him.

"I trust Monsieur has not judged me," she said, "by the unpleasantness of Tuesday evening. I have suffered much on account of it—this is the first time since that evening that I have left my cabin, I have been so ashamed," she concluded simply.

"One does not judge the gazelle by the lions that attack it," replied Tarzan. "I had seen those two work before—in the smoking-room the day prior to their attack on you, if I recall correctly. Having seen them work, I am convinced that any-one they hate must be a person of integrity. Their kind love only what is wicked; they hate all that is noble and good."

"It is very kind of you to put it that way," she replied, smiling. "I have already heard about the matter of the card game from my husband. He spoke especially of the strength and bravery of Monsieur Tarzan, to whom he owes an immense debt of gratitude."

"Your husband?" repeated Tarzan question-ingly.

"Yes. I am the Countess de Coude."

"I am already well repaid, Madame, in know-ing that I have rendered a service to the wife of the Count de Coude."

"Alas, Monsieur, I already am so greatly indebt-ed to you that I can never hope to adequately repay you, so please do not increase my obligations," and she smiled sweetly. In Tarzan's view, a man might easily attempt much greater feats than he yet had, simply for the pleasure of that smile.

"Is it not strange how swift are the friendships of an ocean crossing, Monsieur, and how they are again broken forever with equal ease?"

Tarzan smiled, nodded politely, and continued on his way.

He did not see her again that day, and in the rush of landing on the following morning he missed her entirely, but something in her eyes as they had parted on deck the previous day haunted him. It had been almost wistful.

As he walked onto French soil, Tarzan wondered if he would ever see her again.

CHAPTER 3

What Happened in the Rue Maule

When he arrived in Paris, Tarzan went directly to visit his old friend, Lieutenant Paul D'Arnot of the French Navy. The officer was highly critical of Tarzan's decision to renounce the title and estates that were rightly his from his father, John Clayton, the late Lord Greystoke.

"You must be mad, my friend," said D'Arnot, "to give up not only wealth and title, but also to decline the chance to prove that your blood is that of a nobleman, not that of a savage ape. I cannot understand how any of them could believe you, especially Miss Porter. I myself never did, not even when you tore and ate your meat raw like an animal in the African jungle. Even then, I knew that Kala was not your mother.

"And now we have your father's diary telling of your parents' terrible experiences on that wild African shore; the account of your birth; and, as final proof, your own baby fingerprints in that diary. It seems incredible to me that you choose to remain a nameless, penniless vagabond."

23

"I do not need any better name than Tarzan, and I have no intention of remaining a penniless vagabond," replied the ape-man. "In fact, I hope that you will help me find employment, so that I will no longer need to impose upon your unselfish friendship."

"Pooh, pooh!" scoffed D'Arnot. "Have I not told you a dozen times that I have enough for twenty men, and will gladly give you half? The gift of everything I own could never repay your friendship and your services to me. But for your wondrous bravery, I would have died at the stake in that African village. Nor do I forget that you helped me to recover from the terrible wounds I received there. Only later, when we returned to the coast and found Miss Porter and her party gone, did I discover what that cost you. I am not trying to repay you with money, Tarzan, for I never could. Rather, at present you happen to need money, and my friendship and my money are yours."

"Well," laughed Tarzan, "we shall not quarrel over the money, then. I must have it to live, so I accept. But I shall die of boredom without something to do, so I will be grateful if you can find me employment. As for my birthright, it is in good hands. Clayton did not rob me of it; he truly believes that he is the real Lord Greystoke. He will make a better English lord than a man who was born and raised by apes in an African jungle. You know that, even with all your hard work, I am still only half civilized. A moment of anger, and all my savage instincts take over, brushing aside culture and refinement. What is more, had I claimed my heritage, I would have robbed the woman I love of wealth and position. Could I have done that, Paul?

"Nor is my birth of great importance to me," he continued. "I see no worth in man or beast except what they earn by their own mental or physical abilities. I am just as happy to think of my mother as the kindly she-ape Kala, who actually nursed and raised me, as I am of the noble English girl who gave birth to me and then died a year later. Kala protected me with a real mother's love against the wild creatures of the forest as well as members of our own tribe.

"And I loved her, Paul. I did not realize how much until after the cruel spear and the poisoned arrow had stolen her away from me. I was still a child when that occurred, and I threw myself upon her dead body and wept as any child would weep for his mother. To you, my friend, she would have appeared hideous and ugly, but to me she was beautiful—such is love. So I am perfectly content to remain forever the son of Kala, the she-ape."

"I admire your loyalty," said D'Arnot, "but one day you will be glad to claim what is yours. Let us hope that it will be as easy then as it is now. Bear in mind that Professor Porter and Mr. Philander are the only people in the world who can swear that the little skeleton found in the cabin cradle was that of an infant ape, and not the child of Lord and Lady Greystoke. They are both old men, and they may not live many more years. And did it not occur to you that if Miss Porter knew the truth, she might break her engagement with Clayton? You might easily have your title, your estates, and the woman you love, Tarzan. Had you not thought of that?"

Tarzan shook his head. "You do not know her," he said. "Nothing could bind her closer to her bargain than Clayton's misfortune. She is from an old southern family in America, and southerners pride themselves on their loyalty."

Tarzan spent the next two weeks getting reacquainted with Paris. By day he haunted the libraries and art galleries. He had become a heavy reader, and the world of possibilities amazed him. Not in a lifetime could one human gain even a tiny part of the world's knowledge, but he enjoyed trying. At night, he sought relaxation and amusement, and Paris offered plenty of these. They also helped him to forget the love he had lost and the thought of a future without it.

He was sitting in a music hall one evening, sipping his cocktail and admiring the art of a famous Russian dancer, when he glimpsed a pair of evil black eyes staring at him. The man turned and was lost in the crowd before Tarzan could catch a good look at him, but he recognized those eyes. It was no accident. For some time he had sensed that he was being watched, and in response to this deep animal instinct, tonight he had turned suddenly to surprise the watcher. But before he left the music hall, he had forgotten the matter.

As he left the brilliantly-lit music hall, Tarzan did not notice the swarthy man lurking in the shadows of a doorway. He had been followed more consistently than he realized, but he was usually with D'Arnot. Tonight his friend had other plans, so Tarzan had come alone.

As he turned in his usual direction toward his apartment, the watcher across the street ran from his hiding place and followed at a rapid pace.

Tarzan liked to take the Rue Maule on his way home at night. Its quiet darkness reminded him of his beloved African jungle. The Rue Maule is a narrow, forbidding street and, at night, it is perhaps the most dangerous street in all Paris.

Tonight Tarzan had gone some two blocks through the dense shadows cast by the rundown old tenements when he suddenly heard a woman screaming for help. The call came from a building on the other side of the street. Before the echoes of her first cries had died, Tarzan was on his way to her rescue.

He followed the screams up to the third floor. There, at the end of the corridor, a door stood slightly open, the cries for aid clearly coming from within. Another instant found him in the center of a room, with a single candle casting its dim light over a dozen repulsive figures. All but one were men; the other was a woman of about thirty. She might once have been lovely, but poor living had left its mark on her. She stood with one hand at her throat, crouching against the wall.

"Help, Monsieur," she cried in a low voice as Tarzan entered the room, "they were killing me."

Tarzan quickly examined the men and saw the crafty faces of longtime criminals. How strange that they were making no effort to escape! Then he got a brief glance of Rokoff sneaking out of the room. He recognized him immediately but something else he saw was of more immediate interest. A great brute of a man was tiptoeing up on him from behind with a huge club in his hand.

Just as he noticed the man with the bludgeon, the entire pack rushed Tarzan from all sides with knives, chairs, and fists. The man with the club swung it with enough power to crush Tarzan's head.

But the brain, agility and muscles that had been a match for the mighty strength and cruel craftiness of Terkoz, the great ape, and Numa, the lion, were not to be easy prey for Parisian thugs. Tarzan charged the man with the club, dodged its swing, and felled him in his tracks with a terrific blow on the chin. Then he turned to the others. This was great sport: the joy of battle, the lust of blood. He shed civilization as a snake sheds its

skin. The ten burly crooks found themselves penned up in a small room with a wild beast, against whose muscles their own were puny.

At the end of the corridor outside, Rokoff awaited the outcome. He wished to be sure that Tarzan was dead before leaving, but he planned not to be a witness to the actual murder.

The woman had not moved, but her face had changed expressions several times. It had gone from seeming distress to craftiness, then to surprise and horror. The immaculate gentleman lured by her cries had turned into a demon of revenge. Instead of soft muscles and a weak resistance, she was looking upon a Hercules gone mad.

"Mon Dieu!" she cried, "he is a beast!" With good reason, for the strong, white teeth of the

ape-man had found the throat of one of his assailants, and Tarzan fought as he had learned to fight with the great bull apes of the tribe of Kerchak. He leapt everywhere, with movements like a panther she had seen at the zoo. Here he broke a wrist; now a shoulder was dislocated as he forced an arm upward and backward.

With shrieks of pain the men escaped into the hallway as quickly as they could; but even before the first one staggered bleeding and broken from the room, Rokoff had seen enough to realize that Tarzan would not be the one to die in that house this night. So the Russian hastened to telephone the police, telling them that a man was committing murder on the third floor at 27 Rue Maule.

When the officers arrived they found three men groaning on the floor, a frightened woman lying upon a filthy bed with her face buried in her arms, and what appeared to be a well-dressed young gentleman standing in the center of the room. They were mistaken about the last judgment. What looked at them from those narrowed lids and steel-gray eyes was a wild beast.

"What has happened here?" asked one of the policemen. Tarzan explained briefly, but when he turned to ask the woman to confirm his statement he got a disappointing surprise.

"He lies!" she screamed shrilly at the policeman. "He came to my room while I was alone, and for no good purpose. When I refused him, he would have killed me, but my screams attracted these passing gentlemen. He is a devil, Messieurs; alone he has all but killed ten men with his bare hands and his teeth."

Tarzan was struck mute by her ingratitude. The police were skeptical, for this was not their first dealing with this woman and her lovely group of 'gentlemen.' However, being policemen and not judges, they decided to arrest everyone in the room. A judge would separate the innocent from the guilty.

But it was one thing to tell this well-dressed young man that he was under arrest, and quite another to enforce it.

"I am guilty of no offense," he said quietly. "I have but sought to defend myself. I do not know why this woman has lied to you. She cannot hate me, for until I came to this room in response to her cries, I had never seen her."

"Come, come," said one of the officers; "there are judges to listen to all that," and he advanced to lay his hand upon Tarzan's shoulder. An instant later he lay crumpled in a corner of the room. As his comrades rushed in upon the ape-man, they experienced a taste of the same treatment the criminals had gotten. They did not even have a chance to draw their revolvers.

During the brief fight, Tarzan had noted a tree or a telegraph pole—he could not tell which— out the open window. As the last officer went down, another succeeded in drawing his revolver, and fired at Tarzan from where he lay on the floor. The shot missed, and before the man could fire again Tarzan had knocked the candle over. The room was plunged into darkness. They could barely see his lithe form spring out the open window and onto the pole, then vanish. When the police gathered themselves together and reached the street their prisoner was nowhere to be seen.

In their soreness and humiliation, they were none too gentle as they took the woman and the remaining thugs to the station. They were not going to enjoy having to report that a single unarmed man had beaten them all, then escaped easily. The officer who had remained in the street swore that no one had leaped from the window or left the building while they had been inside. His comrades thought that he lied, but they could not prove it.

In the meantime, when Tarzan found himself clinging to the pole outside the window, he first obeyed his jungle instinct: look before venturing down. Below, there was a policeman; above, there was no one. Up he went. The top of the pole was opposite the roof of the building, and in an instant he was across the gap. He continued in this way from one building to another until he came to another pole. He descended and ran for a block or two, then ducked into a little all-night café and headed for the men's room.

After cleaning up the evidence of his rooftop promenade, he exited and walked casually on toward his apartment building. Near his goal, he came to a well-lit boulevard and prepared to cross. As he stood beneath a brilliant streetlight, waiting to let a limousine pass, he heard his name called in a sweet feminine voice. Looking over, he met the smiling eyes of Olga de Coude as she leaned forward in the back seat of the vehicle. He bowed very low in response to her friendly greeting, but when he straightened up, the machine had borne her away.

"Rokoff and the Countess de Coude, both in the same evening," he mused; "Paris is not so large, after all."

CHAPTER 4

The Countess Explains

"**Y**our Paris is more dangerous than my African jungles, Paul," concluded Tarzan, after telling his friend of his evening's adventures. "Why did they lure me there? Were they hungry?"

D'Arnot laughed. "It is hard to grow used to civilized ways, is it not, my friend?" he bantered.

"Civilized ways, indeed," scoffed Tarzan. "In the jungle, we do not commit wanton acts of violence. There we kill for food and for self-preservation, or to win mates and protect the young. But here! Your civilized man kills for no reason, and worse, he uses the noble sentiment of a cry for help to lure his unwary victim to an ambush. I still cannot understand how any woman could sink so low as to call a would-be rescuer to death. Rokoff must have known that I often walked the Rue Maule. He arranged it all in advance, even the woman's story in case something went wrong. It is all perfectly clear to me."

"Well," said D'Arnot, "among other things, it has taught you something I have been unable to—

that the Rue Maule is a good place to avoid after dark."

"On the contrary," replied Tarzan, with a smile, "it has convinced me that it is the one worthwhile street in all Paris. I shall walk it again every chance I get, for it has given me the first real entertainment I have had since I left Africa."

"It may give you more than you want even without another visit," said D'Arnot. "I assure you that the police of Paris will not soon forget what you did to them. Sooner or later they will get you, my dear Tarzan, and then they will lock the wild man of the woods up behind iron bars. How will you like that?"

"They will never lock Tarzan of the Apes behind iron bars," he replied, grimly.

Something in Tarzan's voice caused D'Arnot to look up sharply at his friend. What he saw in the set jaw and the cold, gray eyes made the young Frenchman fear for this overgrown child, who recognized no law other than his own mighty strength. The police must be dealt with, and soon.

"You have much to learn, Tarzan," he said gravely. "The law must be respected, like it or not. If you defy the police you will have nothing but trouble. I can explain the matter to them once, and I shall do that this very day, but henceforth you must obey the law and the police, no matter what they tell you. Now, let us go to my friend in the department and explain this matter of the Rue Maule. Come!"

Half an hour later, they called on the police official. He was very cordial, and remembered Tarzan from their prior visit concerning finger-prints several months ago.

When D'Arnot finished his story, a grim smile was playing about the lips of the policeman. He touched a button, and as he waited for the clerk to respond, he searched through the papers on his desk until he found the one he wanted.

"Here, Joubon," he said as the clerk entered. "Send for these officers at once," and he handed the man the paper. Then he turned to Tarzan, and spoke gravely but not unkindly.

"You have committed a serious offense, Monsieur, and without the explanation made by your friend here, I would judge you harshly. Instead, I am about to do an unheard-of-thing. I have summoned the officers whom you mistreat-ed. They shall hear Lieutenant D'Arnot's story, and then I shall let them decide whether you shall be prosecuted or not.

"You have much to learn about the ways of civilization. Until you can understand the motives behind them, you must learn to accept things that seem strange to you. The officers you attacked were only doing their duty. Every day they risk their lives to protect the lives and property of oth-ers, as they would do for you. They are very brave men, and they are deeply humiliated by such a defeat.

"Make it easy for them to overlook what you did. You seem a very brave man, and brave men usually have generous hearts."

Now the four policemen appeared. As their eyes fell on Tarzan, they widened in surprise.

"Here, gentlemen," said the official, "is the man whom you met in the Rue Maule last evening. He has come voluntarily to give himself up. Listen attentively to Lieutenant D'Arnot, who will tell you more about Monsieur's life—it may explain his conduct last night. Proceed, my dear lieutenant."

D'Arnot spoke to the policemen for half an hour about Tarzan's wild jungle life. He explained how he had learned the instinct of self-preservation. It was this instinct that had made him attack them, not reason. He had not understood their intentions; thus, as in the jungle, he had assumed them to be enemies.

"Your pride has been wounded," said D'Arnot, in conclusion, "but you need feel no shame. Had you been penned in that small room with an African lion, or with the great gorilla of the jungles, you would not be embarrassed by defeat. Well, gentlemen, the muscles you battled have time and again fought and defeated lions, gorillas and many other terrors of Africa. It is no disgrace to be defeated by superhuman strength."

And then, as the men stood looking from Tarzan to their superior, the ape-man did the one thing which could truly set matters right.

With outstretched hand he advanced. "I am sorry for the mistake I made," he said simply. "Let us be friends."

And that was the end of it, except that Tarzan became a subject of much conversation in the barracks of the police, and he gained four brave men as his friends.

On their return to D'Arnot's apartment, the lieutenant found a letter awaiting him from William Cecil Clayton, Lord Greystoke. The two had kept in touch since their friendship began in Africa. Their ill-fated expedition in search of Jane Porter after her kidnapping by Terkoz, the bull-ape, had drawn them together.

"They are to be married in London in about two months," said D'Arnot, as he finished reading the letter. Tarzan did not need to be told who 'they' were. He made no reply, but he was very quiet and thoughtful all day.

That evening the two men attended the opera. Tarzan paid little attention to the show; his mind was filled with gloomy thoughts. He saw only the lovely vision of a beautiful American girl, and heard only a sad, sweet voice returning his love. And she was to marry another man!

As he struggled to shake off his mood, he felt eyes upon him and looked up—squarely into the shining eyes of Olga, Countess de Coude. As Tarzan returned her bow, he saw an invitation—

perhaps even a plea—in those eyes. At the next intermission, he went to sit in her opera-box.

"Monsieur Jean Tarzan, I have so much wished to see you," she said. "You deserve an adequate explanation as to why we took no steps to prevent future attacks by those two evil men. You must think us deeply ungrateful, and I am troubled by it."

"Of course not," replied Tarzan. "You owe me no explanation, and I think most highly of you. Have the scoundrels annoyed you further?"

"They never cease," she replied sadly. "I feel that I must tell someone, and no one else deserves the truth as much as you. Permit me to do so, for I know Nikolai Rokoff quite well enough to be positive that he will try to take revenge upon you. I wish to give you information that may help you to combat his schemes. I cannot tell you here, but tomorrow evening at five, Monsieur Tarzan may come to my home."

"It will be an eternity until the hour arrives," he said, and bade her good night.

From a corner of the theater Rokoff and Paulvitch saw Tarzan leave the opera-box of the Countess de Coude, and both men smiled.

At four-thirty the following afternoon, a swarthy, bearded man rang the bell at the servants' entrance of the palace of the Count de Coude. The doorman who answered, Jacques, raised his eyebrows in recognition. They spoke quietly; at first Jacques seemed to answer in the negative, but an instant later, something was pressed into his hand. Then he led the visitor to a small alcove off the tearoom where the Countess usually entertained guests.

Half an hour later, Tarzan was ushered into the room, and presently his hostess arrived. "Jean, I am so glad that you came," she said with a smile.

"Nothing could have prevented me," he replied.

For a few moments they spoke of the opera, of the current events in Paris, and of the pleasure of renewing the acquaintance which had begun under such odd circumstances. This brought them to the real reason for their meeting.

"You must have wondered," said the Countess finally, "what Rokoff could hope to gain from harassing us. It is very simple. The Count is entrusted with many of the vital secrets of the Ministry of War. Agents of foreign powers would give a fortune, commit murder or worse, to get their hands on these secrets. Right now he has papers with information that the Russian Czar's government would pay dearly to learn, and Rokoff and Paulvitch are Russian spies who will stop at nothing to get it. The purpose of the affair on the liner was to blackmail my husband into divulging these secrets.

"Had he been thought guilty of cheating at cards, his career would have been ruined. He would have had to leave the Ministry, and he would have been a social outcast. They intended to hold this threat over him. If the Count would give them the papers they seek, they would supposedly have spoken up to protect his reputation.

"You thwarted this plan. Then they came up with a scheme to use my reputation, rather than the Count's, as the price of the papers. Paulvitch explained it to me when he came into my cabin: if I would not get the papers for him, Rokoff would notify the purser that I was entertaining a man not my husband behind locked doors in my cabin. He would tell everyone on the boat, and when we landed, would give the whole story to the newspapers.

"It was horrible," she went on. But I happen to know something about Monsieur Paulvitch. If the police of St. Petersburg were to learn it, Paulvitch would hang. I dared him to carry out his plan, and then I leaned over and whispered a name in his ear. Like that"—she snapped her fingers—"he flew at my throat like a madman. He would have killed me if you had not interfered."

"The brutes!" muttered Tarzan.

"They are worse than that, my friend," she said. "They are devils. I fear for you because they now hate you. Tell me that you will be on your guard constantly, for I could never forgive myself were you to suffer for your kindness to me."

"I do not fear them," he replied. "I have survived nastier enemies than Rokoff and Paulvitch."

She clearly knew nothing of the occurrence in the Rue Maule, and he decided not to distress her with it.

"For your own safety," he continued, "why do you not turn the scoundrels over to the authorities? They would make quick work of them."

She hesitated for a moment before replying.

"For two reasons," she said finally. "One reason keeps the Count from action. The other—my real reason—only Rokoff and I know." She paused, looking intently at him for a long time.

"Even if you are you guilty of murder, Madame, I will not judge you harshly," said Tarzan.

"Oh, dear, no," she exclaimed, "it is not *that* terrible. But first let me tell you why the Count does not prosecute these men; then, if my courage holds, I shall tell you the real reason that I dare not.

"The first is that Nikolai Rokoff is my brother. We are Russians. Nikolai has always been a bad man. He was a captain in the Russian army, but was dismissed after a scandal. After some time, my father obtained a position for him in the secret service.

"Nikolai has been accused of many terrible crimes, but he always manages to escape punishment. Lately he has evaded it by framing people for treason against the Czar, then turning them in to the Russian secret police. They are always quite eager to uncover traitors, and in this eagerness, have accepted his evidence and let him go."

Tarzan looked grim. "You owe him no loyalty, Madame. Haven't his blackmails against you and your husband broken all bonds of kinship?" he asked. "After all, he has sought to stain your honor even though you are his sister."

"Ah, but there is another reason. While I may owe him no loyalty because he is my brother, he knows something else about me that could be embarrassing.

"I might as well tell you everything," she resumed after a pause, "for I obviously need to tell someone. I was educated in a convent. While there, I met a man whom I thought to be a gentleman. I was young and ignorant and thought I was in love. At his urging, I ran off with him, and we were to be married. Imagine my surprise to find the police waiting for us at our destination— they arrested him. It turned out that he was a common deserter and criminal, known to nearly every police department in Europe. I was sent back to the convent, where the matter was hushed up. Not even my parents knew. But Nikolai met the man afterward, and learned the whole story. Now he threatens to tell the Count if I do not obey him."

Tarzan laughed. "You are indeed very young. This story cannot harm your reputation, especially if you go to your husband tonight, and tell him the whole story just as you have told it to me. Unless

I am much mistaken he will put your fears to rest, and take immediate steps to put that precious brother of yours in prison where he belongs."

"I only wish that I dared," she said; "but I am afraid. Men have always frightened me. First there was my father, then Nikolai, then the holy-fathers in the convent. Nearly all my friends fear their husbands—why should I not fear mine?"

"Why should women fear men?" asked Tarzan in puzzlement. "In the jungle, it is more often the other way around. Men were created to protect women. I should hate to think that any woman feared me."

"I do not think that any woman would fear you, my friend," said Olga de Coude softly. "I have not known you for long, yet you are the only man I know that I could never fear. And it is strange, for you are very strong. The ease with which you handled Nikolai and Paulvitch that night in my cabin was marvelous."

She then insisted that he promise to return tomorrow, and they parted soon after. As he left, Tarzan wondered why she wanted another meeting so urgently. Her hand had seemed to cling to his during the parting clasp, and the memory of her lovely smile and eyes remained with him the rest of the day. Olga de Coude was a very beautiful woman, and Tarzan of the Apes a very lonely young man, with a pained heart in need of a woman's care.

As the Countess turned back into the room after Tarzan's departure, she found herself face to face with Nikolai Rokoff..

"How long have you been here?" she cried, shrinking away from him.

"Since before your lover came," he answered, with a nasty leer.

"Stop!" she commanded. "How dare you say such a thing to your sister!"

"Well, my dear Olga, if he is not your lover, accept my apologies. But had he one-tenth the knowledge of women that I have, you would be in his arms this minute. He is stupid, Olga. Why, your every word and act was an open invitation to him, and he lacked the sense to see it."

The woman put her hands to her ears. "I will not listen to the wicked things you say. No matter how you threaten me, you know that I am a loyal woman. After tonight you will not dare to annoy me again, for I shall tell Raoul everything. He will understand, and then, Nikolai, beware!"

"You shall tell him nothing," said Rokoff. "I have caught you in an affair, and with the help of those in your house, there shall be no shortage of sordid details to pour into your husband's ears. And you a trusted wife, Olga. An affair . . . shame on you," and he laughed brutishly.

So the Countess told her Count nothing, and matters were worse than before. The vague fear previously in her mind was now a very real one.

It may also be that a guilty conscience played a part.

CHAPTER 5

The Plot That Failed

For a month, Tarzan was a frequent visitor to the beautiful Countess de Coude. Often he met other members of the select little group that dropped in for tea in the afternoon. More often, Olga found excuses to be alone for an hour with Tarzan.

Nikolai's hints had frightened her. She had not thought of the big young man as anything but a friend, but her brother's evil words made her doubt her own intentions. In reality, she wanted a friend her own age rather than an exchange of love—her husband was twenty years her senior and not easy to confide in. Moreover, Tarzan was decent and honorable, and she felt she could trust him.

From a distance, Rokoff watched this growing friendship with malicious glee. Once he was aware that Tarzan knew him to be a Russian spy, Rokoff feared exposure. Now he waited until the moment was right for the master stroke that would rid him of Tarzan and avenge his humiliations and defeats.

Tarzan was happier than he had been since he first met the marooned Porter party. He enjoyed visiting with Olga's friends, but especially the friendship of the Countess herself. It helped to soothe his lacerated heart. Sometimes D'Arnot went with him, for he had long known both Olga and the Count. The many demands of duty and politics usually kept the Count himself away from home until late at night.

Rokoff spied on Tarzan almost constantly, waiting for him to stop by the de Coude palace at night, but he was disappointed. A few times Tarzan walked the Countess home after the opera, but much to Rokoff's dismay, he always he left her at the entrance. Eventually Rokoff and Paulvitch gave up and hatched another plan.

For days they watched the papers, looking for items on either the Count or Tarzan. Soon they were rewarded: a morning paper made brief mention of a banquet to be given by the German minister, and the Count de Coude was on the guest list. If he attended, he would not return home until after midnight.

On the night of the dinner, Paulvitch waited at the curb in front of the German minister's residence, watching to see who arrived. Before long, de Coude descended from his car and passed him. Paulvitch hastened back to his apartment. There he and Rokoff waited until after eleven, at which time Paulvitch went to their telephone. He called a number.

"Is this the apartment of Lieutenant D'Arnot?"

he asked, when he had been put through.

"A message for Monsieur Tarzan, if he will kindly come to the telephone."

For a minute there was silence, then:

"Monsieur Tarzan?"

"Ah, yes, Monsieur, this is François—in the service of the Countess de Coude. Possibly Monsieur does poor François the honor to remember him?

"Yes, Monsieur. I have an urgent message from the Countess. She asks that you hasten to her at once—she is in trouble, Monsieur.

"No, Monsieur, I do not know. May I assure Madame that Monsieur will be here shortly?

"Thank you, Monsieur. God will bless you."

Paulvitch hung up the receiver and turned to grin at Rokoff.

"It will take him thirty minutes to get there. You can reach the German minister's in fifteen; de Coude should get home in about forty-five minutes. It all depends upon whether the fool will linger after he finds that it is a trick, but unless I am mistaken, Olga will not wish to let him go so soon. Here is the note for de Coude. Hurry!"

Paulvitch hastened back to the German minister's. At the door he handed the note to a footman, saying, "This is a very urgent note for the Count de Coude. You must see that he receives it at once," and he dropped a piece of silver into the willing hand of the servant. Then he returned to his apartment.

A moment later de Coude was apologizing to his host as he tore open the envelope. What he read left his face white and his hand trembling.

MONSIEUR LE COUNT DE COUDE:

One who wishes to preserve your honor warns you that it is in jeopardy this very minute.

A certain man, who for months has been a constant visitor at your home during your absence, is now with your wife. If you go at once to your Countess' bedroom you will find them together.

A FRIEND

Twenty minutes after Paulvitch had called Tarzan, Rokoff phoned Olga's private line. Her maid answered the telephone, which was in the Countess' bedroom.

"But Madame has gone to bed," said the maid, in answer to Rokoff's request to speak with her.

"This is a very urgent message for the Countess's ears alone," replied Rokoff. "Tell her that she must quickly arise, slip something on and come to the telephone. I shall call again in five minutes." Then he hung up his receiver. A moment later Paulvitch returned.

"The Count has the message?" asked Rokoff.

"He should be on his way home by now," replied Paulvitch.

"Good! My lady will be sitting in her bedroom about now, and with luck, in a nightdress. In a minute, the faithful Jacques will escort Monsieur

Tarzan into her presence without announcing him. Explanations will take a few minutes. Olga will look very enticing in her state of partial dress, and she will be surprised but not displeased. If there is a drop of red blood in the man, in about fifteen minutes the Count will burst in on a very pretty love scene. My dear Alexei, we have planned marvelously. Let us go out and drink a toast to Monsieur Tarzan, remembering that the Count de Coude is not only a fine swordsman, but by far the best shot in all of France."

When Tarzan reached the de Coude palace, Jacques awaited him at the entrance.

"This way, Monsieur," he said, and led the way up the broad marble staircase. In another moment he opened a door, drew aside a heavy curtain, and bowed Tarzan into a dimly lit room. Then he vanished.

Across the room, Tarzan saw Olga seated at a little desk in front of her telephone, fidgeting impatiently. She had not heard him enter.

"Olga," he said, "what is wrong?"

She turned toward him with a little cry of alarm. "Jean!" she cried. "What are you doing here? Who admitted you? What does it mean?"

Tarzan was thunderstruck, but in an instant he realized a part of the truth. "Then you did not send for me, Olga?"

"Send for you at this time of night? *Mon Dieu!* Jean, do you think me insane?"

"François telephoned me, saying that you were in trouble and wanted me to come at once," Tarzan explained.

"François? Who in the world is François?"

"He said that he was in your service. He spoke as though I should remember him."

"No one by that name works for me. Someone has played a joke on you," and Olga laughed.

"I fear that it may be a most sinister joke, Olga," he replied. "There is more behind it than humor."

"What do you mean? You do not think that—"

"Where is the Count?" he interrupted.

"At the German ambassador's."

"This is another move by your brother. Tomorrow the Count will hear of it, and will question the servants. Everything will point to—to what Rokoff wishes the Count to think."

"The scoundrel!" cried Olga. She had arisen, and come close to Tarzan, where she stood looking up into his face, terrified. Trembling, she raised her hands to his broad shoulders to steady herself. "What shall we do, Jean?" she whispered. "It is terrible. Tomorrow all Paris will read of it—he will see to that."

It was the ancient appeal of a frightened woman to her natural protector—a man. Tarzan took a warm little hand in one of his own, and without really thinking about it, put the other arm about her shoulders.

The result was electrical. They had never before been so close together. In startled guilt they looked suddenly into each other's eyes, and where Olga de Coude should have been strong she was weak and she nestled closer. And Tarzan of the Apes? He took the panting figure into his mighty arms, and covered her hot lips with kisses.

Meanwhile, after reading the note from the 'friend,' Raoul de Coude made hurried excuses to his host and left. Later it was all a blur to him, up to the moment he reached his own doorstep. Then he became very cool, moving with caution. Only later did he recall that Jacques had so quickly opened the door for him.

Very softly he tiptoed up the stairs toward his wife's bedroom. In his hand was a heavy walking stick; in his heart was murder.

Olga was the first to see him. With a horrified shriek she tore herself from Tarzan's arms, and the ape-man turned just in time to ward off a terrific blow aimed at his head. Once, twice, three times the heavy stick fell, and each blow pushed the ape-man a step closer to the jungle.

With the low snarl of the bull ape he sprang for the Frenchman. The great stick was torn from his grasp and broken like matchwood, then flung aside. The infuriated beast's next move was for his attacker's throat.

Olga de Coude watched in horror for a moment, then sprang to where Tarzan was strangling the Count, shaking him as a terrier shakes a rat. Frantically she tore at his great hands. "Mother of God!" she cried. "You are killing him! Oh, Jean, you are killing my husband!"

Tarzan was deaf with rage. Suddenly he hurled the body to the floor and placed his foot on the upturned chest. He raised his head, and then, throughout the palace, rang the awesome challenge of the bull ape after a kill. Every servant in every corner of the house trembled. The woman in the room sank to her knees beside the body of her husband and prayed.

Slowly the red mist faded from before Tarzan's eyes, and he became once again a civilized man. His eyes fell upon the kneeling woman. "Olga," he whispered. She looked up, expecting to see the maniacal light of murder in the eyes above her. Instead she saw sorrow and apology.

"Oh, Jean!" she cried. "Look at what you have done. He was my husband. I loved him, and you have killed him."

Very gently Tarzan raised the limp form of the Count de Coude and carried it to a couch. Then he put his ear to the man's breast. "Some brandy, Olga," he said.

She brought it, and together they forced it between his lips. Presently a faint gasp came from them. The head turned, and de Coude groaned.

"He will not die," said Tarzan. "Thank God!"

"Why did you do it, Jean?" she asked.

"I do not know. He struck me, and I went mad, as I have seen the apes of my tribe do. I have never told you my story, Olga. It would have been better had you known it—this might not have happened.

"I never met my father. The only mother I knew was a ferocious she-ape. Until I was fifteen I had never seen a human being. I was twenty before I saw a white man. A little more than a year ago I was living as a naked beast of prey in an African jungle.

"Do not judge me too harshly. Two years is too short a time in which to abandon the savage habits of a lifetime."

"I do not judge at all, Jean. The fault is mine. You must go now—he must not find you here when he awakes. *Adieu!*"

It was a sorrowful Tarzan who walked with bowed head from the palace of the Count de Coude. Soon his thoughts took shape, and he went to a police station just off the Rue Maule. Here he found one of the officers who had tried to arrest him several weeks before. The policeman greeted him warmly, and after an exchange of pleasantries, Tarzan asked if he had ever heard of Nikolai Rokoff or Alexei Paulvitch.

"Very often, indeed, Monsieur. Each has a police record, and though neither is charged with anything right now, we keep tabs on their whereabouts as we do with every known criminal. Why does Monsieur ask?"

"I know them also," replied Tarzan. "I wish to see Monsieur Rokoff on a little matter of business. If you can direct me to his lodgings I shall appreciate it."

A few minutes later, with an address in his pocket, he bade the policeman *adieu* and looked for a taxi.

Rokoff and Paulvitch had returned to their rooms, and were discussing the probable outcome of the evening's events. They had phoned the offices of one of the morning papers. At any moment they expected a reporter to arrive, eager for the juicy scandal that would rock the Paris social scene the next day.

A heavy step sounded on the stairway. "Ah, but these newspaper men are prompt," exclaimed Rokoff, as a knock sounded on the door. He said, "Enter, Monsieur."

The smile of welcome froze upon the Russian's face as he looked into the hard, gray eyes of his visitor.

"You dog!" he shouted, springing to his feet. "What brings you here, of all people?"

"Sit down!" said Tarzan, in a low tone that brought Rokoff to his chair and kept Paulvitch in his.

"You know what has brought me here," he continued, in the same low tone. "It should be to kill you, but because you are Olga de Coude's brother I shall not do that—yet.

"I shall give you a chance for your lives. Paulvitch is merely a stupid little tool, so I will not kill him unless I choose to kill you, Rokoff. Before I leave you two alive in this room, you will have done two things. The first will be to write a full confession of your roles in tonight's plot—and sign it. The second will be to promise me, upon pain of death, that none of this will get into the newspapers.

"If you break your promise, you will both die the next time I pass through that doorway. Do you understand?" Then, without waiting for a reply: "Start writing. *Now!*"

Rokoff's expression and posture were defiant, as if to show fearlessness. An instant later he felt the ape-man's steel fingers clamp about his throat. Paulvitch attempted to dodge around them toward the door, but was lifted completely off the floor and hurled senseless into a corner with a crash. When Rokoff started to turn purple, Tarzan released his hold and shoved the fellow back into his chair.

After a moment of coughing, Rokoff sat sullenly glaring at the ape-man. Presently Paulvitch came to and limped painfully back to his chair at Tarzan's command.

"Now write," said the ape-man. "If it is necessary to handle you again, I shall be rough."

Rokoff picked up a pen and commenced to write. "See that you omit no detail or name," cautioned Tarzan.

Presently there was a knock at the door. "Enter," said Tarzan.

A dapper young man came in. "I am from the newspaper *Le Matin*," he announced. "I understand that Monsieur Rokoff has a story for me."

"Then you are mistaken, Monsieur," replied Tarzan courteously. "You have no story for publication, have you, my dear Nikolai?"

Rokoff looked up from his writing with an ugly scowl upon his face. "No," he growled, "I have no story for publication—now."

"Nor ever, my dear Nikolai," and the reporter did not see the deadly light in the ape-man's eye. Rokoff did.

"Nor ever," he repeated hastily.

"I am sorry that Monsieur has been misinformed," said Tarzan, turning to the newspaperman. "Good evening, Monsieur," and he bowed the well-dressed young man out of the room and closed the door.

An hour later Tarzan, with a rather bulky manuscript in his coat pocket, turned at the door leading from Rokoff's apartment.

"If I were you I would leave France," he said, "for sooner or later I shall find an excuse to kill you that will not in any way disturb your sister."

CHAPTER 6

The Duel

D'Arnot was asleep when Tarzan returned from Rokoff's apartment, so Tarzan waited until morning to tell him the whole story of the previous evening.

"What a fool I have been," he concluded. "De Coude and his wife were both my friends, and how have I repaid them? I nearly murdered the Count, I have shamed the Countess, and I have probably broken up a happy home."

"Do you love Olga de Coude?" asked D'Arnot.

"No, Paul. For an instant we were overcome by madness, which would have soon passed even had de Coude not returned. As you know, I have little experience with women. Olga de Coude is very beautiful; the surroundings were seductive. She was defenseless and appealing to me for protection. A more civilized man might have resisted, but my civilization is not even skin deep—it ends at my clothes.

"Paris is too restrictive for me, my friend, with all its man-made rules and pitfalls. I feel like a prisoner. I think I should go back to my own jungle, to live as God intended me to live when He put me there."

"Tarzan, you take it too harshly," responded D'Arnot. "You handled yourself better under the circumstances than many 'civilized' men would have. As for leaving Paris, I suspect that Raoul de Coude may have something to say about that before long." With that, his voice grew solemn.

Nor was D'Arnot mistaken. A week later, an impressively polite gentleman named Monsieur Flaubert called at their apartment during breakfast. He had the honor to be Monsieur le Count de Coude's second, he said. With many low bows he delivered the Count's challenge to Monsieur Tarzan: "Would Monsieur kindly arrange for a friend to meet with me soon to arrange the details of the duel?"

"Certainly," replied Tarzan. "I would be delighted to have my friend, Lieutenant D'Arnot, serve as my second." It was arranged that D'Arnot would call on Monsieur Flaubert at two that afternoon, and bowing politely, Flaubert took his leave.

When they were again alone, D'Arnot looked quizzically at Tarzan. "Well?"

"Now I must either add murder to my sins or be killed myself," said Tarzan. "I am becoming very civilized."

"As the one challenged, the choice of weapons is yours. What weapons shall you select?" asked D'Arnot. "De Coude is a master with the sword, and a splendid shot."

"Then perhaps poisoned arrows, or spears, at twenty paces," laughed Tarzan. "Make it pistols, Paul."

"He will kill you, my brave Jean."

"I have no doubt of it," replied Tarzan. "I must die someday."

"We had better make it swords," said D'Arnot. "He will be satisfied with wounding you, with less danger of a mortal wound."

"Pistols," said Tarzan, with finality. Nothing D'Arnot said could change his mind. At the appointed time, therefore, D'Arnot went, and returned from his conference with Monsieur Flaubert shortly after four.

"It is all arranged," he said. "Tomorrow morning at daylight, at a secluded spot on the road not far from Etamps. For some personal reason Monsieur Flaubert preferred it, and I agreed."

"Good!" was Tarzan's only comment, and he did not again refer to the matter that day.

That night he wrote several letters before bedtime. After sealing and addressing them, he placed them all in an envelope addressed to D'Arnot. As he prepared for bed, D'Arnot heard him humming a music-hall tune. The Frenchman swore inwardly. His friend was sure to die tomorrow, and did not even seem to care.

D'Arnot awakened him from a comfortable bed before daylight. "This is a most uncivilized hour for people to kill each other," remarked the ape-man. He had slept well.

D'Arnot had not, and was in no mood for jokes. "I presume you slept like a baby all night," he said.

Tarzan laughed. "From your tone, Paul, you seem to hold it against me. I could not help it, really."

"No, Jean; it is not that," replied D'Arnot, smiling despite himself. "But your indifference is most exasperating. One would think that you were going out target-shooting, rather than to face one of the best shots in France."

Tarzan shrugged. "I am going out to atone for a great wrong, Paul. My opponent's good aim is required for my atonement. Why should I be dissatisfied? Have you not told me that Count de Coude is a splendid marksman?"

"You mean that you hope to be killed?" exclaimed D'Arnot, in horror.

"Not precisely, but you must admit that I probably will be killed."

Had D'Arnot known what had been in the ape-man's mind—almost from the first hint that de Coude would issue a challenge—he would have been even more horrified.

Neither spoke as they sped over the dim road leading to Etamps, each man deep in his own thoughts. D'Arnot mourned inside. The two men's lives and experiences were so different, but the common ideals of manhood, bravery and honor had united them. He was proud to call Tarzan his friend.

For his part, Tarzan of the Apes was wrapped in the more pleasant memories of his lost jungle life. He recalled the countless hours he had spent in his father's cabin, learning to read the fascinating picture books. A smile of contentment softened his strong face as he thought of that one special day alone with Jane Porter deep in the forest.

Presently his thoughts were interrupted by the braking of the car—they had arrived. Tarzan was unafraid. Like all jungle creatures, he had seen much death. The law of nature compels them to fight for life, but not to fear death.

D'Arnot and Tarzan were first on the field of honor. A moment later de Coude, Monsieur Flaubert, and a third gentleman arrived—a doctor.

D'Arnot and Monsieur Flaubert whispered together briefly. Together the seconds examined both pistols, loading each with three bullets while the Count de Coude and Tarzan stood at opposite sides of the field. Presently the seconds summoned them, and both duelists stood silently while Monsieur Flaubert recited the rules:

"Gentlemen, we shall first ask that you stand back to back. I will give a signal, upon which you are to kindly walk ten paces in opposite directions with your pistols at your sides. The esteemed Lieutenant shall keep track, and when you have both done so, he shall give the final command. Then you may turn and fire at will, until one should fall, or until both pistols are empty."

While Monsieur Flaubert spoke, Tarzan listened casually. De Coude was perfectly cool, for he was the best shot in France.

Presently Monsieur Flaubert nodded to D'Arnot, and each of the seconds armed and positioned his principal.

"Are you quite ready, gentlemen?" asked Monsieur Flaubert.

"Quite," replied de Coude.

Tarzan nodded. Monsieur Flaubert gave the signal. He and D'Arnot stepped back a few paces to be out of the line of fire as the men paced slowly apart to D'Arnot's count.

"Six! Seven! Eight!"

There were tears in D'Arnot's eyes. He loved Tarzan very much.

"Nine!"

Another pace, and the poor lieutenant gave the signal he so hated to give, the doom of his best friend: "Ten! *Turn and fire!*"

Quickly de Coude wheeled and fired. Tarzan gave a little start. His pistol still dangled at his side. The Count waited to see his target crumple—he could not have missed.

Still Tarzan made no move to raise his pistol. De Coude fired once more, but the indifference of the ape-man had rattled the best marksman in

France. This time Tarzan remained motionless, but again de Coude knew that he had hit.

Suddenly the Count realized: his enemy was taking these cool chances in the hope that none of the three shots would seriously wound him. He would then take his time, deliberately and coolly shooting de Coude down in cold blood. A little shiver ran up the Frenchman's spine. This was diabolical. What manner of creature was this that could stand calmly with two bullets in him, waiting for the third?

And so de Coude took careful aim this time, but his nerve was gone, and he missed cleanly. Not once had Tarzan raised his pistol.

For a moment the two looked straight into each other's eyes. Tarzan's were sorrowful; de Coude's were terrified. Soon he could endure it no longer. "Mother of God! Monsieur—shoot!" he screamed.

But Tarzan did not raise his pistol. Instead, he advanced toward de Coude. Both seconds misinterpreted his intention, and rushed between them, but he raised his left hand. "Do not fear," he said to them, "I shall not harm him."

It was highly unusual, but they halted. Tarzan advanced very near to de Coude.

"There must have been something wrong with Monsieur's pistol," he said. "Or Monsieur is nervous. Take mine, Monsieur, and try again," and Tarzan offered his pistol, grip first, to the astonished de Coude.

"Mon Dieu, Monsieur!" cried the de Coude. "Are you mad?"

"No, my friend," replied the ape-man, "but I deserve to die. Only in that way can I atone for the wrong I have done a very good woman. Take my pistol and do as I ask."

"It would be murder," replied de Coude. "But what wrong did you do my wife? She swore to me that—"

"I do not mean that," said Tarzan quickly. "No wrong was done but what you saw. But that was enough to dishonor her name and to ruin the happiness of a decent man. The fault was all mine, and so I hoped to die for it this morning. Unfortunately, Monsieur's marksmanship has been overrated."

"You say that the fault was all yours?" asked de Coude eagerly.

"All mine, Monsieur. Your wife loves only you. The thing that brought me there was neither her fault nor mine as this paper will explain." Tarzan drew from his pocket Rokoff's signed confession.

De Coude took it and read. D'Arnot and Monsieur Flaubert had drawn near, interested in this strange ending to a strange duel. No one spoke until de Coude had quite finished. Then he looked up at Tarzan.

"You are a very brave and chivalrous gentleman," he said. "I thank God that I did not kill you." Impulsively, he threw his arms about Tarzan in an embrace, and Monsieur Flaubert embraced D'Arnot, as Frenchmen do.

Perhaps the doctor was miffed that there was no one to embrace him, for he interfered, demanding to dress Tarzan's wounds. "This gentleman was hit once at least," he said. "Possibly more."

"Twice," said Tarzan. "Once in the left shoulder, and again in the left side—both flesh wounds, I think." But at the doctor's insistence, he lay down while he cleansed and dressed both injuries. They all rode back to Paris together in D'Arnot's car as friends.

Despite his objections, the ape-man was confined to his bed for several days on the doctor's orders and with D'Arnot's firm enforcement. "This is silly," Tarzan told him. "I lie bedridden with a scratch! Why, when Bolgani, the king gorilla, tore me almost to pieces, I had no nice soft bed to lie on—only the damp floor of the jungle, with only faithful Kala to nurse and protect me. When I called for water she brought it to me in her own mouth—the only way she could carry it. There was no sterile gauze, there was no bright white bandage—it would have driven our dear doctor mad—yet I recovered. And now I lie in bed because of a tiny scrape that no jungle beast would bother to notice."

But Tarzan was soon up and about. De Coude had visited several times, and when he was reminded that Tarzan wanted a job, he promised to see what could be found. On Tarzan's first day out, he received a message asking him to stop by the Count's office that afternoon.

He found de Coude waiting for him with a very pleasant welcome, sincerely glad that he was recovered. Neither had spoken of the incident or the resulting duel, since their meeting on the field of honor.

"I think that I have found just the thing for you, Monsieur Tarzan," said the Count. "It requires great trust, physical strength and courage. I cannot imagine a better man for it. It will require travel, and may later lead to a better job—possibly in the diplomatic service.

"At first, for a short time only, you will be a special agent of the Ministry of War. Let me take you to General Rochère, who will be your chief. He can explain the duties better than I, and then you may accept or decline."

De Coude escorted Tarzan to the general's office, and gave him a glowing description of Tarzan's fitness for the work. He then left them alone for the interview.

A half hour later, Tarzan walked out of the office with the first job of his life. He was to return the next day for instructions, though General Rochère had made it plain that Tarzan should prepare to leave Paris—perhaps as soon as tomorrow.

Elated, he hastened home to tell D'Arnot the good news. At last he was to be of some value in the world! He was to earn money, and, best of all, to travel and see the world. He could scarcely wait to get inside D'Arnot's sitting room before he burst out with the glad tidings.

D'Arnot was not so pleased. "You seem delighted that you are to leave Paris, and that we may not see each other for months. Tarzan, you are a most ungrateful beast!" and he laughed.

"No, Paul; I am a little child. I have a new toy, and I am tickled to death."

And so, on the following day, Tarzan left Paris for Marseilles. He would sail from there to Oran in Algeria.

He was going back to Africa.

CHAPTER 7

The Dancing Girl of Sidi Aïssa

Tarzan's first mission looked to be rather dull and unimportant at the start.

French North Africa was garrisoned partly by *spahis*, Arab light cavalry with French officers. A certain Lieutenant Gernois, of the *spahis*, was under suspicion. He had recently served on the general staff headquarters at Sidi-bel-Abbès, Algeria, where he had access to secret material. He was suspected of trading those secrets to another European power. A jealous woman in Paris had tipped off the French authorities, and the army's general staff takes a dim view of treason. Tarzan had been sent to Algeria, posing as an American hunter, to keep a close eye on Lieutenant Gernois.

Tarzan had looked forward with delight to seeing his beloved Africa again, but this part of Africa was so different from his tropical jungle that he might as well have been back in Paris. At Oran he spent a day wandering the narrow, crooked alleys of the Arab quarter, enjoying the strange new sights. Then he went to Sidi-bel-Abbès and presented his letters of introduction to the authorities—but without revealing his mission. His English was good enough to convince both Arabs and Frenchmen that he was American.

He soon became well liked by many of the French officers. He met Gernois, whom he found to be a standoffish, sour-tempered man who kept to himself. For a month nothing important occurred; Gernois had no visitors, nor any suspicious contacts when he went to town. Tarzan was beginning to hope that the rumor might have been false after all.

Then suddenly Gernois's troop of *spahis* was ordered to Bou Saada, in the Petit Sahara far to the south, to relieve another unit stationed there. Fortunately another of the officers, Captain Gerard, had become a close friend of Tarzan's. When the ape-man asked if he might accompany the horsemen to Bou Saada, where there might be good hunting, it caused no suspicion at all. They would go by train as far as Bouira, then continue south on horseback.

When they reached Bouira, Tarzan went shopping for a mount. While he was negotiating with the horse-trader, he caught a glimpse of someone in European clothing eyeing him from the doorway of a coffeehouse. Something seemed familiar about him, but Tarzan gave it no more thought.

The southward ride was tiring to a man of

Tarzan's limited riding experience, so he checked into a hotel while the troop bedded down at a military post at Aumale. The *spahis* were ready to ride on early the next morning, and Tarzan had to wolf down his breakfast in order not to be left far behind.

As he was finishing, he glanced into the hotel bar. To his surprise, there was Gernois, in conversation with the very stranger the ape-man had seen in the coffee-house at Bouira the previous day. As his eyes lingered on the two, Gernois happened to notice Tarzan's scrutiny. Immediately he interrupted the stranger's whispers, and the two moved out of Tarzan's sight. Maybe they were up to something—such guilty behavior was worth watching.

A moment later Tarzan entered the barroom, but the men had left. He looked around the street for them in vain and then rode south to catch up with the soldiers. He did not overtake the troop until he found them resting at the little town of Sidi Aïssa shortly after noon. Here he found Gernois with the troop, but there was no sign of the stranger.

It was market day at Sidi Aïssa; many caravans of camels were coming in from the desert, and the marketplace was crowded with robed Arabs doing business. Tarzan wanted to learn more of these desert people, so he informed the captain of his desire to stay for a day or so. The cavalrymen continued on south without him.

He spent the day wandering around the market accompanied by a young Arab interpreter/guide, Abdul, who had been recommended by the innkeeper as trustworthy. Here he bought a better mount than the one he had purchased at Bouira. While negotiating, he learned the seller's identity: he was Kadour ben Muhammad, the sheik of a desert tribe. Through Abdul, Tarzan invited the trader to dinner.

As the three were making their way through the crowds of people, camels, donkeys and horses, Abdul plucked at Tarzan's sleeve. "Look, master, behind us," and he turned, pointing at a figure who disappeared behind a camel just as Tarzan turned. "He has been following us all afternoon," continued Abdul.

"I caught only a glimpse of an Arab in a dark-blue robe and white turban," replied Tarzan. "Is that who you mean?"

"Yes. He is not from here. An honest Arab would have something better to do than to sneak around that way, and also, he hides the lower part of his face. He is up to no good."

"He is on the wrong scent then, Abdul," replied Tarzan, "for no one here even knows me. This is my first visit to your country. He will soon discover his error, and stop following us."

"Unless he is planning robbery," returned Abdul.

"Then all we can do is wait until he tries it,"

laughed Tarzan, "and now that we are ready for him, he will get all the robbing he could ever want." After that, he put the mystery man out of his mind—for now.

They had an agreeable dinner, and Kadour ben Muhammad prepared to take courteous leave of his host. He invited his new friend Tarzan to come visit his tribe and go hunting. There was plenty of wild game, said the Arab trader, to tempt a good hunter. They parted on excellent terms.

After this, the ape-man and Abdul again wandered into the streets of Sidi Aïssa, where he was soon attracted by the wild mix of sounds coming from a number of open doorways. "What kind of place is that?" asked Tarzan, indicating one.

"It is called a 'Moorish café,' master. They provide Arab dining and entertainments."

"I have never been in one. Let us go in."

It was after eight, and the dancing was in full swing as Tarzan entered. The room was filled with Arabs, smoking and drinking thick, hot coffee. Tarzan and Abdul found seats near the center of the room, though the quiet-loving ape-man would rather have been farther away from the loud Arab drums and pipes. An attractive girl in a colorful dress, adorned with gold and silver jewelry, was dancing. Seeing in Tarzan's European clothes a generous tip, she threw her silken handkerchief on his shoulder, and he tipped her a franc.

When another dancer took her turn, the

sharp-eyed Abdul saw the first girl in conversation with two Arabs across the room near a side door leading to a small courtyard. At first he thought nothing of it, but then he saw one of the men nod in their direction. The girl shot a discreet glance at Tarzan. The Arab men melted through a nearby doorway.

The first girl's turn to dance came again, and she hovered close to Tarzan, favoring him with the sweetest smiles. This brought many an ugly scowl from the crowd, but Tarzan paid no attention. Again she cast her handkerchief and was rewarded with a franc. As she tucked it away, she bent to whisper to Tarzan.

"There are two men outside in the courtyard," she said quickly in broken French, "who would harm M'sieur. I promised to lure you to them, but you have been kind, and I cannot. Go quickly, before they find that I have deceived them. I think that they are very bad men." Tarzan thanked the girl and assured her that he would be careful. After her dance, she crossed to the little doorway and went out into the courtyard.

But Tarzan did not leave the café as she had urged. For another half hour nothing unusual occurred; then, a surly-looking Arab entered the café from the street. He stood near Tarzan, saying something about him in Arabic. Tarzan had no idea of his meaning until Abdul spoke up.

"This fellow and others are looking for trouble," warned the boy. "In fact, in case of a disturbance, nearly every man here would be against you. It would be better to leave quietly, master."

"Ask the fellow what he wants," commanded Tarzan.

Abdul did so. "He says that 'the dog of an unbeliever' insulted the dancing-girl, who belongs to him. He means trouble, M'sieur."

"Tell him that I did not insult his or any other girl, that I wish him to leave me alone, and that he and I have no quarrel."

Abdul translated this, then the reply: "He says that not only are you a dog, but that you are the son of one, and that your grandmother was a hyena, and furthermore, he calls you a liar."

Now the exchange had the attention of those

nearby. The sneering laughs left no doubt as to whose side they were on. Tarzan did not like being laughed at, nor did he like the Arab's insults, but he arose with no sign of anger—even smiling. Then suddenly, with all his strength, he drove his mighty fist into the Arab's face.

As the man fell, half a dozen angry men sprang into the room on cue. With cries of "Kill the unbeliever!" and "Down with the infidel dog!" they made straight for Tarzan. The dancers all fled upstairs. A number of the younger Arabs in the audience sprang to their feet to join in the assault.

Tarzan and Abdul were forced back by sheer numbers as the young Arab drew a knife to fight loyally at the ape-man's side. It seemed impossible that either could survive, for their many enemies were armed with wicked-looking swords and knives, but the room was too crowded for most of the weapons to be used. With tremendous blows, Tarzan felled all who came within his reach, fighting silently and with a smile.

Finally he succeeded in seizing one of his most persistent attackers, and disarmed him with a quick wrench. Placing the Arab in front of him as a shield, he and his young guide backed toward the door to the inner courtyard. At the doorway he paused, lifted his struggling shield overhead, then hurled him forcefully into the group attacking them. Then Tarzan and Abdul stepped into the semidarkness of the courtyard, lit only by the candles in the windows of the dancing-girls' rooms above.

They were scarcely through the doorway when a revolver went off from the shadows near them, and as the two turned to meet this new attack, a second masked figure sprang toward them and also fired. Tarzan leaped, and the first man lay a second later in the trampled dirt, disarmed, groaning from a broken wrist. The second placed his pistol to Abdul's head and pulled the trigger, but it misfired. The faithful young man's knife found his vitals, and man and revolver fell to the ground.

The maddened horde within the café were now rushing out in pursuit into the nearly pitch dark courtyard. Tarzan seized the sword from the man Abdul had stabbed, and stood waiting in the shadows for the rush of men.

Suddenly he felt a light hand upon his shoulder from behind. A woman's voice whispered, "Quick, M'sieur; this way! Follow me."

"Come, Abdul," said Tarzan, in a low tone, to the youth; "anywhere she leads us will be better than staying here!"

The woman turned and led them up the narrow stairway that led to her quarters, Tarzan close beside her. He realized that she was the same dancer who had warned him earlier. As they reached the top of the stairs, they could hear the angry crowd searching the courtyard below.

"Soon they will search here," whispered the

girl. "Though you fight with the strength of many men, they will kill you in the end. Hurry! You can drop from the far window of my room to the street below. Before they discover that you are no longer in the courtyard you will be safe inside your hotel."

Even as she spoke, several men had started up the stairway. There was a sudden cry from one of the searchers—Tarzan and Abdul had been discovered. Quickly the crowd rushed for the stairway.

The lead attacker leaped quickly upward, but at the top he met the sudden unexpected stroke of a sword. With a cry, the man toppled backward, knocking the rest of the attackers downstairs. With a creaking and rending of breaking wood, the ancient, rickety staircase collapsed beneath the Arabs, leaving Tarzan, Abdul, and the girl alone on the frail platform at the top.

"Come!" she cried. "They will reach us from another stairway through the room next to mine. We have not a moment to spare."

Just as they were entering the room Abdul translated a cry from the yard below: "Some men have been ordered to cut off our escape through the street."

"We are lost now," said the girl simply.

"We?" questioned Tarzan.

"Yes, M'sieur," she responded; "they will kill me as well for having aided you."

This changed matters. Up to now, Tarzan had

been rather enjoying the excitement and danger. He had not stopped to think that either Abdul or the girl could suffer except by accident. Alone, he probably could have fought his way through the mob to an easy escape. Now he must think of these two faithful friends.

He crossed to the window overlooking the street. In a minute there would be enemies below. Already he could hear the mob clambering up the stairway to the next quarters—they would soon be at the door. He put a foot upon the window sill and leaned out, but he did not look down. Above him, within arm's reach, was the low roof of the building. He called to the girl to come and stand beside him; then he put his great arm around her and lifted her up across his shoulder.

"Wait here until I reach down for you from above," he said to Abdul. "In the meantime, push everything in the room against that door." Then, with the girl draped on his shoulders, he stepped to the sill of the narrow window while Abdul hastily shoved furniture. "Hold tight," he cautioned her, and a moment later he had clambered to the roof above. Setting the girl down, he leaned far over the roof's edge and called softly to Abdul. The youth ran to the window.

"Your hand," whispered Tarzan. The men in the room beyond were battering at the door. With a sudden crash it splintered in, and at the same instant Abdul felt himself lifted like a feather onto the roof above. They were not a moment too soon, for as the men broke into the room, a dozen more rounded the corner in the street below and came running to a spot beneath the girl's window.

CHAPTER 8

The Fight in the Desert

As the three squatted on the roof above the dancers' quarters, Abdul translated the angry cursing from the room beneath.

"They are cursing those in the street below," said Abdul, "for letting us escape so easily. The others reply that we are still inside the building. They accuse those above of being too cowardly to attack us, and of lying to them. In a moment they will be brawling among themselves."

Presently the men gave up the search and returned to the café. A few remained in the street below, smoking and talking.

"Thank you," said Tarzan to the girl. "Why did you aid a total stranger?"

"I liked you," she said simply. "You were unlike the others who come to the café, who often insult me. You spoke politely to me."

"What shall you do after tonight?" he asked. "You cannot return to the café. Can you still be safe in Sidi Aïssa?"

"Tomorrow it will be forgotten," she replied.

"But I would be glad never to return. It was never my choice—I have been a prisoner."

"A prisoner!" exclaimed Tarzan in shock.

"A slave, really," she answered. "I was kidnapped from my father's village two years ago by bandits, who brought me here and sold me to the owner of this café. My own people are very far to the south, and never come to Sidi Aïssa."

"If you would like to return to your people, then I promise to see you safely at least as far as Bou Saada. There we can arrange with the commandant to send you the rest of the way."

"Oh, M'sieur," she cried, "how can I ever repay you! You cannot mean that you will do so much for a poor dancing girl. But my father will reward you, for he is the great sheik, Kadour ben Muhammad."

"Kadour ben Muhammad!" exclaimed Tarzan. "Why, he is in Sidi Aïssa this very night. We dined together, in fact."

"My father in Sidi Aïssa?" cried the amazed girl. "Allah be praised! I am indeed saved."

"Hssh!" cautioned Abdul. "Listen."

From below came the sound of voices, clear in the still night air. The girl translated: "They have gone now. It is you they want, M'sieur. A stranger had offered them money to kill you, but now he lays in bed with a broken wrist. However, he offers an even greater reward if they will ambush and kill you on the road to Bou Saada."

"It is the man who followed M'sieur around the market today," exclaimed Abdul. "I saw him in the café with another man, and the two went out into the courtyard after talking with this girl. It was they who attacked us as we came out. Why do they wish to kill you, M'sieur?"

"I do not know," replied Tarzan, and then, after a pause: "Unless—" But he did not finish. The only possible answer seemed too far-fetched

Presently the men in the street went away, leaving the courtyard and the café deserted. Cautiously, Tarzan lowered himself to the windowsill. The room was empty. He returned to the roof and let Abdul down to the sill, then he lowered the girl into his Arab guide's arms.

From the window Abdul dropped the short distance to the street below, while Tarzan took the girl in his arms and leaped down. A little cry of alarm was startled from the girl's lips, but Tarzan landed gently in the street and set her safely down on her feet.

She clung to him for a moment. "How strong and agile M'sieur is," she cried. "*El-Adrea*, the black lion himself, is no stronger."

"I should like to meet this *El-Adrea*," he said. "I have heard much about him."

"If you come to my father's village, you shall," she said. "He lives in the mountains north of us, and comes down at night to hunt. A single blow of his paw can crush the skull of a bull, and the traveler who meets *El-Adrea* at night is doomed."

They reached the hotel without further trouble. The sleepy landlord did not want to search for Kadour ben Muhammad until the following morning, but Tarzan was unwilling to wait. A gold coin changed hands, and a servant was sent out to search.

After perhaps half an hour, the messenger returned with a very curious Kadour ben Muhammad. "Monsieur has done me the honor to—" he began, and then his eyes fell upon the girl. With outstretched arms he crossed the room to meet her. "My daughter!" he cried. "Allah is merciful!" and tears dimmed the eyes of the old warrior.

When the story of her abduction and her final rescue had been told to Kadour ben Muhammad he extended his hand to Tarzan.

"All that is Kadour ben Muhammad's is yours, my friend, even his life," he said very simply, but Tarzan felt the sincerity of the words.

They decided that despite the sleepless night, it would be best to start early in the morning and attempt to reach Bou Saada in one day. It would be tiring for the girl, but she was the most eager for it—she would reach her family and friends that much sooner.

It seemed to Tarzan that he had barely closed his eyes before he was awakened, and in another hour they were headed south toward Bou Saada. For a few miles the road was good, but it soon gave way to a sandy waste. The horses' hooves sank deep with every step. They were accompanied by the sheik's four armed escorts. If all went well, they would reach Bou Saada before nightfall.

A brisk wind enveloped them in the blowing sand of the desert until Tarzan's lips were parched and cracked. The surrounding country was a vast expanse of barren little hills, tufted here and there with clumps of dreary shrub. Far to the south rose the dim lines of the Saharan Atlas Mountains. How different, thought Tarzan, from the lush Africa of his boyhood!

The ever-alert Abdul looked backward almost as often as he looked ahead. At the top of each hill he would turn and carefully scan behind them. At last his alertness was rewarded. "Look!" he cried. "There are six horsemen following us."

"Your friends of last evening, no doubt, Monsieur," remarked Kadour ben Muhammad dryly to Tarzan.

"No doubt," replied the ape-man. "I am sorry that my presence endangers you. At the next village, I shall remain and question these gentlemen while you ride on. I need not reach Bou Saada tonight, and I wish you to ride in peace."

"If you stop we shall stop," said Kadour ben Muhammad. "Until you are safe with your friends, or the enemy has left your trail, we shall remain with you. There is nothing more to say."

Tarzan nodded his head. Like Kadour ben

Muhammad, he was a man of few words.

As the day went on Abdul continued to watch the horsemen in their rear. They did not attempt to get closer, even during the party's rest stops. "They are waiting for darkness," said Kadour ben Muhammad.

Darkness came with Bou Saada just visible in the distance. Sure enough, Abdul's last sight of the pursuers before dusk was of them rapidly gaining. To avoid alarming the girl, he whispered the fact to Tarzan.

"Ride ahead with the others, Abdul," said Tarzan. "This is my quarrel. I shall wait at the next convenient spot, and interview these fellows."

"Then Abdul shall wait at thy side," replied the young Arab. No threats or commands could move him from his decision.

"Very well, then," replied Tarzan. "Here atop this little hill is a good place. We shall hide in these rocks, and when they appear, we will have questions for them."

They dismounted. The others, riding ahead, were already out of sight in the darkness. Beyond them shone the lights of Bou Saada. Tarzan readied his rifle and revolver, and ordered Abdul to take the horses behind the rocks out of harm's way. The young Arab pretended to obey, but when he had secured the animals to a low shrub he crept back to lie on his belly a few paces behind Tarzan.

The ape-man stood up in the middle of the

road, waiting. He did not have long to wait before the sound of galloping horses came suddenly out of the darkness below him, and a moment later he identified the light-robed forms of mounted men.

"Halt," he cried, "or we fire!"

The figures came to a sudden stop, and for a moment there was silence. Then came the sound of a whispered discussion, and like ghosts the phantom riders dispersed in all directions. The desert was still again, but with an ominous sense of evil.

Abdul raised himself to one knee. Tarzan cocked his jungle-trained ears, and presently he heard horses walking quietly through the sand on all sides, surrounding them. Then a shot came from the direction in which he was looking, a bullet whirred through the air above his head, and he fired at the flash of the enemy's gun.

Instantly the desert exploded into the quick rattle of constant gunfire. Abdul and Tarzan could only fire at the flashes, which seemed to be growing nearer. Their enemies had begun to realize that they faced only two men.

One came too close, for Tarzan's eyes were used to the darkness of the jungle night. He fired, and with a cry of pain a saddle was emptied.

"The odds are evening, Abdul," said Tarzan, with a low laugh.

But not even enough. When the five remaining horsemen whirled at a signal and charged them, the battle looked grim. Both Tarzan and

Abdul sprang to the shelter of the rocks to keep the enemy in front of them. There was a mad clatter of galloping hooves, then another exchange of shots. Now only four Arabs remained mounted, and they withdrew to repeat the maneuver.

For a few moments no sound came from the darkness. Tarzan could not tell whether the Arabs had given up the fight, or had moved to a new ambush position south toward Bou Saada.

Before long he had his answer, for now, all from the south, came the sound of a new charge. But scarcely had the first gun spoken when a dozen shots rang out behind the attackers. With them came the wild shouts of a new party, and the sound of many horses pounding toward the area from the direction of Bou Saada.

The marauding Arabs did not wait to see who was coming. With a parting volley as they rode by Tarzan and Abdul, they plunged off along the road toward Sidi Aïssa.

A moment later Kadour ben Muhammad and his men dashed up. The old sheik was much relieved to find that neither Tarzan nor Abdul had received a scratch, nor had their horses. They sought out the two men Tarzan had shot, but finding both of them dead, they left them where they lay.

"Why did you not tell me that you were going to ambush those fellows?" asked the sheik in a hurt tone. "We might have had them all if the seven of us had stopped to meet them."

"Then it would have been useless to stop at all," replied Tarzan, "if we had simply ridden on toward Bou Saada, we would have been fighting them all eventually. I did not want my quarrel with them to affect you, and more so, I did not wish your daughter needlessly exposed to gunfire."

Kadour ben Muhammad shrugged his shoulders. He did not enjoy being cheated out of a fight.

The sounds of the little battle so close to Bou Saada had brought out a company of soldiers to investigate. Tarzan and his party met them just outside the town. The officer in charge halted them to ask for an explanation.

"A handful of bandits," replied Kadour ben Muhammad. "They attacked two of our number who had dropped behind, but when we came back, they fled, leaving two of their own dead. None of my party was injured."

This seemed to satisfy the officer, and after taking the names of the party he marched his men on to collect and identify the dead.

Tarzan spent the next two days entirely with Kadour ben Muhammad and his daughter. This race of stern, dignified warriors fascinated him, and he enjoyed learning the basics of their lives, customs and language. Here were people after his own heart! Their wild lives were filled with danger, and appealed to the ape-man in a way that the great, soft cities of civilization could not. With these people, he could be near the wild nature that he loved, yet live with real men and women whom he could honor and respect. Perhaps when his mission was done, he would resign from the Ministry and go to live the rest of his life with the tribe of Kadour ben Muhammad.

When the two days were done, Kadour ben Muhammad and his party prepared to ride south through the pass below Bou Saada. Tarzan rode with them as far as the pass. "My friend, I extend again to you the hospitality of my village," said the grateful sheik. "Please accompany us."

"Yes, by all means, please do so!" encouraged his daughter.

Tarzan smiled warmly, but thought first of Gernois and the strange recent events. "Unfortunately, I have other pressing duties now. But when those duties are done, I promise to come if I can."

"I understand," said Kadour ben Muhammad. "When you come, we shall show you a proper Arab welcome!" They exchanged fond farewells, and parted.

Tarzan sat on his horse at the opening to the pass, gazing after them until they were gone from sight. Then he turned his horse's head and rode slowly back to Bou Saada.

He was staying at the Hotel du Petit Sahara, the front of which had a bar adjoining two dining rooms. One was reserved for the officers of the garrison. After seeing off the sheik's party early in the morning, Tarzan headed back to the hotel and went into the bar while the guests were still at breakfast.

Glancing casually into the officers' dining room, Tarzan spotted something interesting. Lieutenant Gernois was sitting there. A white-robed Arab approached, bent to whisper something into his ear, and went out of the building.

By itself, the incident meant nothing. But when the Arab bent to speak to Gernois, his robe had parted, and Tarzan had noticed something very odd.

The Arab's left arm was in a sling.

CHAPTER 9

Numa *El-Adrea*

Returning to Bou Saada, Tarzan first sent Abdul on back to Sidi Aïssa with the outgoing mail and supply caravan. He pressed a generous payment into his hand, and told him to keep his horse. "Your service has been excellent, Abdul. Take care of your family."

"Allah be praised," replied the young Arab. "I will never forget you, and my family will pray for your safety always." Tarzan watched another friend go.

Also that same day, Tarzan got a letter from D'Arnot. It opened an old wound that Tarzan would have gladly forgotten. But he was not sorry that D'Arnot had written, for he mentioned one topic of eternal interest to the ape-man. He wrote:

MY DEAR JEAN:

Since I last wrote you I went to London on business for three days. The very first day I quite unexpectedly came upon an old friend of yours—none other than Mr. Samuel T. Philander. He insisted that I return to the hotel with him, and there I found the others—

Professor Archimedes Q. Porter, Miss Porter, and Esmeralda.

While I was there, Clayton came in. They are to be married soon; I suspect that we shall receive announcements almost any day now. On account of his father's death, it is to be a very quiet affair—only blood relatives. While I was alone with Mr. Philander, the old fellow confided to me that Miss Porter had already postponed the wedding three times. He thought that she was not particularly anxious to marry Clayton at all, but this time it seems likely that she will go through with it.

Of course, they all asked about you, but I respected your wishes regarding your true origin, and only spoke to them about your present affairs.

Miss Porter was especially interested in news of you, and asked many questions. I am afraid I took a rather unworthy delight in describing your desire to return to your native jungle. I was sorry afterward, for she seemed pained to picture you returning to such dangers. "And yet," she said, "I do not know. Perhaps for Monsieur Tarzan it is not a sad fate, for he loves the restful quiet and beauty of his jungle. You might find it strange, but at times I myself long to return. Those now seem some of the happiest moments of my life, despite my frightening experiences."

She seemed very sad. I suspect that this was her way of sending you a last tender message from a heart that still cares about you, even if it is given to another.

Clayton appeared uneasy while you were the subject of conversation, yet he spoke very kindly of you. I wonder if he suspects the truth?

Tennington, Clayton's good friend, came in with him. He is setting out on yet another cruise in his yacht, and wanted the entire party to join him. He tried to get me to come along, as well—he is thinking of sailing all round Africa. I told him that his precious toy would wind up at the bottom of the ocean one of these days if he kept mistaking his yacht for an ocean liner or a battleship.

I returned to Paris yesterday, met the Count and Countess de Coude at the races. They inquired after you. De Coude seems quite fond of you, and harbors no ill will. Olga is as beautiful as ever, but a trifle subdued. I imagine that she learned a good lesson about life from her encounter with you. It is fortunate for them both that it was you and not another man. Had you sought her love, it could only have brought tragedy.

She asked me to tell you that Nikolai left France after she paid him twenty thousand francs to go and stay away. He had threatened to kill you at the first opportunity, and she is congratulating herself for preventing the attempt. She is very fond of you, and has no doubt that you would kill Nikolai first. She said she would hate for you to have her brother's blood on your hands. The Count agreed, saying that it would take a regiment of Rokoffs to kill you.

I have been ordered back to my ship. She sails from Le Havre in two days under sealed orders. If you write to me in care of her, your letter will eventually reach me. I shall write you again as soon as I can.

Your sincere friend,
PAUL D'ARNOT

"I fear," mused Tarzan, half aloud, "that Olga has thrown away her twenty thousand francs." He read the part about Jane several times. It made him pathetically happy, but it was better than lonely sorrow.

The following three weeks were uneventful. On several occasions Tarzan saw the mysterious Arab with the injured arm, and once again he saw him exchanging words with Lieutenant Gernois. Despite his efforts, Tarzan could not determine where the Arab lived, so he could learn no more. Gernois had been even more distant from Tarzan since the episode in the dining room of the hotel at Aumale. When they did happen to meet socially, his attitude had been snide.

To maintain his cover story, Tarzan spent considerable time hunting gazelle around Bou Saada. He spent entire days in the foothills, but he never shouldered his rifle. He saw no sport in slaughtering a defenseless creature just for fun, and he did not need the food. He always hunted alone, so that no one would learn that it was a sham.

And once, probably because he rode alone, he nearly lost his life. He was riding slowly through a little ravine when a shot sounded close behind him, and a bullet passed through the cork helmet he wore. Although he turned at once and galloped rapidly to the top of the ravine, there was no sign of any enemy, nor of another human being until he reached Bou Saada.

"Yes," he said to himself in recalling the occurrence, "Olga has indeed wasted her twenty thousand francs."

That night he was Captain Gerard's guest at a little dinner.

"Your hunting has not been very fortunate?" questioned the officer.

"No," replied Tarzan; "the game hereabout is timid, nor do I care particularly about hunting game birds or antelope. I think I shall move on farther south, and have a try at some of your Algerian lions."

"Good!" exclaimed the captain. "We are marching toward Djelfa tomorrow, and you may come with us. Lieutenant Gernois and I are to take a hundred men and patrol a district in which bandits are causing a lot of trouble. Possibly we may have the pleasure of hunting the lion together— what do you say?"

Tarzan was more than pleased, and said so, but the captain would have been astonished by the real reason for this. Gernois was sitting opposite the ape-man, and did not seem pleased at all.

"You will find lion hunting more exciting than gazelle shooting," remarked Captain Gerard, "and more dangerous."

"Even gazelle shooting has its dangers," replied Tarzan. "Especially when one goes alone, as I learned today. I also found that while the gazelle is the most timid of animals, it is not the most cowardly." He let his glance pass casually over Gernois, but only briefly. A dull red crept up Gernois' neck, confirming Tarzan's suspicions. Satisfied, the ape-man changed the subject.

When the *spahis* rode south from Bou Saada the next morning there were half a dozen mounted Arab civilians bringing up the rear.

"They are not attached to the command," replied Gerard in response to Tarzan's query. "They merely ride with us for company."

Tarzan had learned enough about Arab tendencies since arriving in Algeria to know that this was not their real motive, for they were never fond of the French military and preferred to steer clear. He decided to keep a sharp eye on them, but they trailed too far behind the column for a closer look.

He had long been sure that hired assassins were hunting him, and that Rokoff was probably behind it. Whether it was to avenge his past humiliations by Tarzan, or had something to do with Gernois's questionable loyalties, Tarzan could not be sure. If it was the latter, then he had two powerful enemies to deal with, and the wilds of Algeria offered many opportunities for easy assassination.

The troop of *spahis* camped at Djelfa for two days. On the second evening, Captain Gerard ordered Lieutenant Gernois to prepare the column to move southwest. About a half hour after this, Tarzan spotted Gernois talking with one of the Arabs who had been following them.

That night, the little band of Arabs suddenly disappeared. Tarzan asked among the Arab cavalrymen, but none could tell him anything about where they might have gone. Tarzan did not like the look of it. The *spahis* had been told only to prepare to break camp and ride; only Gernois and Gerard knew where they were going. Could Gernois have revealed their destination?

They rode off the next morning as planned. Late that afternoon they camped at a little oasis. Here lived a sheik and his tribe, whose flocks were being stolen and whose herdsmen were being killed. The villagers came out of their goatskin tents and asked many questions of the Arab troopers in their native tongue. After a while, the sheik came out to pay his respects to Captain Gerard.

Tarzan had learned enough Arabic to question one of the younger men accompanying the sheik: "No," said the young man, "I have seen no such party riding from the direction of Djelfa. Maybe they were journeying to another oasis. Also, the bandits in the mountains sometimes ride to Bou Saada in small parties, even to Aumale and Bouira. Maybe it was a few of the bandits returning from a pleasure trip to the city." Tarzan thanked him, and returned to camp.

Early the next morning Captain Gerard split his command, giving Lieutenant Gernois command of one section, while he headed the other. They were to scour the mountains on opposite sides of the plain.

"And with which detachment will Monsieur Tarzan ride?" asked the captain. "Or maybe Monsieur does not care to hunt marauders?"

"Oh, I shall be delighted to go," Tarzan responded. He was wondering what excuse he could make to accompany Gernois. To his surprise, Gernois himself came to his rescue.

"If my captain will forego the pleasure of Monsieur Tarzan's company for this once, I shall esteem it an honor indeed to have Monsieur ride with me today," he said with odd warmth. Tarzan did not miss the change in tone, but was quick to agree.

And so Lieutenant Gernois and Tarzan rode off side by side at the head of one section of *spahis*. Gernois' friendliness vanished the instant they were out of Captain Gerard's sight and he became his usual disagreeable self. They advanced into the mountains via a little canyon; the terrain grew rougher. At midday, Gernois called a halt by a little stream for the men to eat a frugal lunch and refill their canteens.

After an hour's rest, they advanced again up the canyon to a spot where several rocky gorges led in different directions up into the mountains. Gernois ordered: "We shall separate here, to explore each of these gorges," and then he divided his squads among the Arab sergeants who would command them. When he was done he turned to Tarzan. "Monsieur will be so good as to remain here until we return."

"I would prefer not to stay," demurred Tarzan.

The officer cut him short. "There may be fighting," he said, "and troops cannot be burdened by civilians during action."

"But, my dear lieutenant," disagreed Tarzan, "I am most ready to obey your orders or those of your sergeants, and to fight in the ranks. It is what I came for."

"I am sure," retorted Gernois, with an undisguised sneer. "Since you are under my orders, I order you to remain here until we return, and not to debate the matter further." With that he turned and spurred away at the head of his group of men. At the same time, the other detachments departed. A moment later Tarzan found himself alone in a desolate mountain valley.

The sun was hot, so he tethered his horse in the shelter of a nearby tree and sat. Gernois had played a mean trick on him. Then it occurred to him: Gernois was no fool. He would not annoy Tarzan in a petty way just for spite; there must be some other motive. He removed his rifle from the boot on the saddle, loaded it, and inspected his revolver. He then kept an eye out, determined not to be caught napping.

The sun sank lower and lower, yet there was no sign of returning *spahis*. Dusk came, but Tarzan was too proud to head back to camp just yet. Night closed in, and he felt safer, for in darkness his security depended upon his strengths: good night vision, sensitive ears, and a highly developed sense of smell. Lulled into security, he fell asleep with his back against the tree.

He must have slept for several hours, for when he was suddenly awakened by the frightened antics of his horse, the moon was shining bright and full. Ten paces before him stood the grim cause of the horse's terror.

Superb, majestic, and with his graceful tail extended and quivering, stood Numa *El-Adrea*: the fabled black lion, with his two eyes of fire riveted on his prey. A little thrill of joy tingled through Tarzan's nerves. It was like a reunion with an old friend.

For a moment he sat still to appreciate the magnificent sight—but not for long. Numa was crouching for the spring. Very slowly Tarzan raised his gun to his shoulder. He had never before killed a large animal with a gun—only with his spear, his poisoned arrows, his rope, his knife, or his bare hands. In fact, he would have preferred his arrows and knife.

Numa was lying quite flat upon the ground now, only his head showing. Tarzan wanted to shoot from the side, for he knew how much damage Numa could do even in his final minute of desperate life with a direct attack. The horse trembled in fear behind Tarzan.

The ape-man took a cautious step to one side. Numa's eyes followed him. Another step, then another; Numa had not moved. Now he could aim at a point between the eye and the ear.

His finger tightened on the trigger, and as he fired Numa sprang. At the same instant the terrified horse made a last frantic effort to escape. The rope broke, and he went galloping down the canyon toward the desert.

Numa *El-Adrea* would have killed any ordinary man with such a spring. Tarzan, however, was quicker than ordinary men. Instead of feeling his claws in soft flesh, the black lion slammed into the tree behind his prey. The 'prey' took a couple of steps to the right and pumped another bullet into the lion, then two more in quick succession. Soon *El-Adrea*'s roars ceased and he lay still.

Tarzan was no longer Monsieur Jean Tarzan. It was Tarzan of the Apes that put a savage foot upon the body of his kill, raised his face to the full moon, and lifted his mighty voice in the terrible victory call of the bull ape. The wild things of the mountains halted their hunting and trembled at this new and awful voice. Down in the desert, its human children came out of their goatskin tents to wonder what new, terrible predator had come to plague them.

A half mile from Tarzan, about twenty white-robed figures were moving. They carried outdated, long, wicked-looking guns. They halted at the sound and looked at one another with questioning eyes, but when it was not repeated, they resumed their stealthy travel toward the valley.

Tarzan was now confident that Gernois was not coming back, but he had no idea why the officer had just left him free to return to camp. His horse gone, it seemed foolish to remain in the mountains, so he set out toward the desert.

He had barely set forth when the first of the robed men entered the valley on the opposite side of the canyon. For a moment they scanned to make sure the depression was empty, and then they advanced. Near the tree they came across the body of *El-Adrea*, and there were muttered exclamations before they set out again down the canyon.

They moved cautiously and silently, using cover, as do men who are stalking men.

CHAPTER 10

Through the Valley of the Shadow

As Tarzan walked down the wild canyon beneath the brilliant African moon, the solitude and the savage freedom filled his heart with life. He was Tarzan of the Apes again—every sense alert against ambush—yet walking proudly, conscious of his might. Some of the sounds of the mountains were new to him, but some were familiar—yes, there was the distant cough of Sheeta, the leopard—or perhaps it was a panther.

Presently a soft, stealthy new sound mingled with the others. No human ears other than Tarzan's would have detected it. Soon he realized that it came from the bare feet of a number of human beings behind him. He was being stalked.

In a flash he knew why Lieutenant Gernois left him in that little valley.

As it was, there had been a hitch in the arrangements—the men were late. Closer and closer came the footsteps. Tarzan halted and faced them, his rifle ready in his hand.

Now he caught a fleeting glimpse of a white

robe. He called aloud in French, "What do you want of me?"

His reply was the flash of a long gun, and with the sound of the shot, Tarzan of the Apes fell forward on his face.

The Arabs waited cautiously to be sure that their victim did not rise. After a time they came out and inspected; he was not dead. One of the men put the muzzle of his gun to the back of Tarzan's head to finish him, but another pushed it aside. "If we bring him alive, the reward is greater," he explained.

So they bound his hands and feet, and four of them shouldered him. The march resumed. When they were out of the mountains they headed south, and at about daylight they came to where two of their number had been left to take care of their horses. After that their progress was rapid. Tarzan had come around and found he was tied to a spare horse, evidently brought along for that purpose. His wound was but a slight scratch across the temple, but his face was smeared with dried blood. He did not speak, nor did the Arabs say much to him.

For six hours they rode rapidly across the burning desert, avoiding the oases along the way. About noon they halted at a camp of about twenty tents.

As one of them began to untie the ropes holding Tarzan on his horse, the group was surrounded by a mob of men, women and children. Many of the tribe, especially the women, seemed to delight in heaping insults on the prisoner and physically abusing him with stones and sticks. Soon an old sheik appeared and drove them away.

"Ali-ben-Ahmed tells me," he said, "that this man sat alone in the mountains and slew *El-Adrea*. I know not why the stranger sent us after him, nor what he will do with him, nor do I care. But this prisoner is a brave man, one who hunted and killed the black lion. While he is here, he will be treated with the respect he deserves."

Tarzan had heard of the regard Algerian Arabs had for a lion-slayer, and he was glad that it had spared him the petty torments. Shortly thereafter he was taken to a goatskin tent, fed, and left lying tightly bound and alone on a piece of native carpet. Tarzan could see a guard outside the tent, but a quick test of the ropes showed that no guard was needed. Not even his giant strength could break them.

Just before dusk several robed men entered the tent where he lay. Presently one of them advanced to Tarzan's side, and the ape-man saw the evil face of Nikolai Rokoff contorted in a nasty smile.

"Ah, Monsieur Tarzan," he said, "this is indeed a pleasure. But why do you not rise and greet your guest?" Then he snarled, "Get up, you dog!" and drew back his booted foot and kicked

Tarzan heavily in the side. "And here is another, and another, and another," he continued, as he kicked Tarzan about the face and side. "One for each of the injuries you have done me."

The ape-man made no reply. He did not even give the Russian the satisfaction of a second glance. Finally the frowning sheik grew disgusted with the cowardly attack, and he commanded: "Stop! Kill him if you will, but no brave man is treated like this in my village. I should turn him loose, and see how long you would kick him then."

This threat put a sudden end to Rokoff's brutality. "Very well," he replied to the Arab; "I shall kill him presently."

"Not within my village," returned the sheik. "When he leaves here, he leaves alive. What you do with him in the desert is none of my concern, but I shall not have the blood of a Frenchman on the hands of my tribe for your sake. They would send soldiers here to kill many of my people, and burn our tents and drive away our flocks."

"As you say," growled Rokoff. "I'll take him out into the desert below the camp and dispatch him."

"You will take him a day's ride from my country," said the sheik, firmly, "and some of my children shall follow you to see that you obey me—otherwise there may be two dead Frenchmen in the desert."

Rokoff shrugged. "Then I shall have to wait

until tomorrow—it is already dark."

"As you will," said the sheik. "But by an hour after dawn you must be gone from my village. I have little liking for unbelievers, and none at all for a coward."

Rokoff bit off a retort. The old man would be all too pleased to turn on him. Together they left the tent, but at the door Rokoff could not help flinging a parting taunt at Tarzan. "Sleep well, Monsieur," he said, "and pray well, for tomorrow you will suffer too badly to do anything but swear."

No one had bothered to bring Tarzan either food or water since noon, and he was very thirsty. He asked his guard for water two or three times, but got no reply and gave up.

Far up in the mountains he heard a lion roar. "How much safer one is," he thought, "in the haunts of wild beasts than in the haunts of men. Never in all my jungle life have I been more relentlessly hunted than in the past few months among civilized men. No one would be tying up Numa the lion, to slaughter him like a sheep with no chance to fight."

It must be near midnight, thought Tarzan. He had several hours to live. Possibly he would yet think of a way to take Rokoff down with him. He heard the roar of *El-Adrea* again, nearer now; perhaps the lord of the desert would raid the village.

For a long time silence reigned, then Tarzan's trained ears caught the sound of a quietly moving body. Nearer and nearer it came. For a time there was a terrible silence; Tarzan was surprised that he did not hear the breathing of the animal that surely must be nearing the back wall of his tent.

He heard it move again, closer. Tarzan turned his head toward the sound. He saw the back of the tent rising from the ground. The head and shoulders of a body blocked out the dim starlight for a moment. The ape-man smiled grimly. Rokoff would be cheated and how infuriated he would be! Tarzan thought at least this death would be merciful.

Now the back of the tent dropped into place, and all was dark again within. Whatever it was, it was inside. He heard it creeping close beside him, and he closed his eyes to await the mighty paw. Instead, on his upturned face was the gentle touch of a soft hand groping in the dark.

A girl's voice whispered: "M'sieur, the strong Frenchman?"

"Yes, it is I," he whispered in reply. "But who in the world are you?"

"The dancing-girl of Sidi Aïssa," came the answer. While she spoke, Tarzan could feel her working to release his bonds. Occasionally the cold steel of a knife touched his flesh. A moment later he was free.

"Come!" she whispered.

On hands and knees he followed her out of the tent. She crawled flat on the ground until she reached a little patch of shrub, then halted until he caught up. For a moment he looked at her before he spoke.

"Why are you here?" he said at last. "How did you know that I was a prisoner in that tent? How have you come to save me?"

She smiled. "I have come a long way tonight," she said, "and we have a long way until we are out of danger. Come! I shall tell you on the way." Together they rose and set off across the desert in the direction of the mountains.

"I was not quite sure that I would ever reach you," she said at last. "*El-Adrea* is abroad tonight, and after I left the horses I think he was on my trail—I was terribly frightened."

"What a brave girl," he said. "And you ran all that risk for a stranger—an unbeliever?"

She drew herself up very proudly. "I am the daughter of the Sheik Kadour ben Muhammad," she answered. "I should be no fit daughter of his if I would not risk my life to save the man who saved my own while he thought I was but a common dancing-girl."

"Nevertheless," he insisted, "you are very brave. But how did you know that I was a prisoner?"

"A cousin of mine on my father's side was visiting some friends in that village, and saw you brought in as he was preparing to leave. When he reached home, he was telling us about the big Frenchman who had been captured by Ali-ben-Ahmed for another Frenchman who wished to kill him. From the description I knew that it must be you.

"My father was away. I tried to persuade some of the men to come and save you, but they said: 'Let the unbelievers kill one another if they wish. It is none of our affair, and if we interfere with Ali-ben-Ahmed's plans we shall only stir up a fight with our own people.'

"So when it was dark I came alone, riding one horse and leading another for you. They are tethered not far from here. By morning we shall be within my father's village. He should be there himself by now—then let them come and try to take a friend of Kadour ben Muhammad."

For a few moments they walked on in silence.

"We should be near the horses," she said. Then she cried out in annoyance: "This is where I tethered them. They are gone!"

Tarzan stooped to examine the ground. A large shrub had been uprooted. Then he found something else, and rose with a wry smile.

"*El-Adrea* has been here. From the signs, though, I think his prey escaped him. With a little start, in the open, horses could outrun him."

There was nothing to do but continue on foot. The way led them across a low spur of the mountains, but the girl knew the trail as well as she did her mother's face. They walked in easy, swinging strides, Tarzan letting her set the pace. As they walked and talked, they occasionally stopped to listen for sounds of pursuit.

It was now a beautiful, crisp, moonlit night. The date palms and goatskin tents stood out behind them. In front of them were the grim, silent mountains. Tarzan's blood leaped in his veins. This was life! He looked down upon the girl beside him, a daughter of the desert walking across it with a son of the jungle, and smiled. He wished that he had a sister like this girl. What a great friend she would have been!

They had entered the mountains now, and were progressing more slowly, for the trail was steeper and very rocky.

For a few minutes they had been silent. The girl was hoping to reach her father's tents before the pursuit caught up. They had just turned around a projecting rock when they were brought to a sudden stop. There before them, in the middle of the path, stood Numa *El-Adrea*, the black lion. His green eyes looked very wicked; he bared his teeth and swished his tail. Then he roared out his anger and hunger.

"Your knife," said Tarzan to the girl, extending his hand. She slipped the hilt of the weapon into his waiting palm. As his fingers closed around it, he drew her back and pushed her behind him. "Walk back to the desert as rapidly as you can. If you hear me call, you will know that all is well, and you may return."

"It is useless," she replied, resignedly. "This is the end."

"Do as I tell you," he commanded. "Quickly! He is about to charge." The girl dropped back a few paces, where she stood awaiting the terrible sight.

The lion was advancing slowly toward Tarzan, his nose to the ground like a challenging bull, and his tail quivering with intense excitement.

The ape-man stood, half crouching, the long Arab knife glistening in the moonlight. Behind him the girl remained tensely still, eyes wide. Her only thought was wonder at the bravery of the man who dared face *El-Adrea*, the black lion, with a puny knife. Any of her brothers would have knelt in prayer and gone down beneath those awful fangs without resistance. In either case the result would be the same, but she could not repress a thrill of admiration as her eyes rested upon the heroic figure before her. His frame did not shake at all—he was as defiant and menacing as *El-Adrea* himself.

The lion was quite close to him now, but a few paces away. He crouched, and then, with a deafening roar, he sprang.

CHAPTER 11

John Caldwell, London

When Numa *El-Adrea* pounced, he expected this puny human to be the same sort of clumsy, easy prey as the twenty other men he had hunted. Imagine his surprise when his mighty leap found his victim no longer in that spot.

The girl could only watch in astonishment. And now, O Allah! He rushed in behind *El-Adrea's* shoulder even before the beast could turn, and grasped his mane. The lion reared up, horse-fashion, as Tarzan had known he would. A giant arm encircled the beast's throat, and once, twice, a dozen times a sharp blade darted in and out of the ebony side behind the left shoulder.

Numa leapt frantically, and roared in awful rage and pain, but nothing could dislodge the giant on his back. Soon Tarzan of the Apes arose from the immense, lifeless body.

Then the daughter of the desert witnessed something even more frightening than the black lion. The man placed a foot upon his kill, raised his handsome face toward the full moon, and voiced the most frightful cry that she had ever heard. She gave a little cry of fear and shrank away.

As the last note of that fiendish challenge echoed away in the distance, Tarzan dropped his eyes to meet hers with a kindly smile on his face. Reassured that he was still sane, she relaxed and smiled back.

"What kind of man are you?" she asked. "This is unheard of. Even now I cannot believe that a lone man defeated *El-Adrea* with only a knife and without a scratch. And that cry—it was not human. Why did you do that?"

Tarzan blushed. "I sometimes forget that I am a civilized man. When I kill, I suppose that I am another creature." He did not try to explain further, for he always expected that a woman would loathe him if she knew just how much of the beast remained within him.

They moved on. The sun was just up when they came out into the desert again. They found the girl's horses grazing beside a little stream, caught them easily, and rode off toward the village of Sheik Kadour ben Muhammad.

At about nine o'clock they reached their destination. The sheik had just returned. He was frantic with grief at the absence of his daughter, whom he thought had been kidnapped again, and had already saddled up fifty men to search for her. His joy at her safe return was only equaled by his gratitude to Tarzan, and his thankfulness that she had been in time to save him. When the girl had recited the story of the slaying of *El-Adrea*, the admiration and respect of the Arabs was cemented.

The old sheik insisted that Tarzan stay. He even wished to adopt him into the tribe, and the ape-man seriously considered accepting. He and these wild people understood each other, and he certainly enjoyed the girl's friendship. Had she been a man, he probably would have stayed. As it was, the strict rules of the tribe regarding men and women would keep them separated forever. Soon she would surely be married to one of these fierce warriors, and that would end their friendship. So he decided against the sheik's proposal, but he lingered for a week as their honored guest.

When he left, Kadour ben Muhammad and fifty white-robed warriors prepared to escort him to Bou Saada. While they were mounting up, the girl came to bid farewell to Tarzan.

"I have prayed that you would remain with us," she said simply, as he leaned from his saddle to clasp her hand in farewell, "and now I shall pray that you will return." There was a wistful expression in her beautiful eyes. Tarzan was touched.

"Who knows?" he said, then turned and rode after the departing Arabs.

He bade Kadour ben Muhammad and his men good-bye outside Bou Saada, for as he had explained to the sheik, he wanted to enter the town as secretly as possible. The sheik agreed that the escort would enter ahead of him. Tarzan would come in later, alone and after dark, and lodge at an obscure inn. He did so unnoticed, and then, after secretly dining as the guest of Kadour ben Muhammad, he took a roundabout way to his former hotel and came in through the back entrance.

The innkeeper seemed very surprised to see him alive. Yes, there was mail for Monsieur; he would fetch it. No, he would mention Monsieur's return to no one. Presently he returned with a packet of letters. One was an order from General Rochère, ordering him to stop investigating Gernois and hasten to Cape Town, in the British colony of South Africa, by the first available ship. There he was to get further instructions from another agent, whose name and address were included. That was all.

Tarzan arranged to leave Bou Saada early the next morning. Then he went to see Captain Gerard, whom the hotel owner said had returned with his *spahis* the previous day. The captain was surprised and pleased to see Monsieur Tarzan alive and well.

"When Lieutenant Gernois returned, he reported that you had chosen to remain behind while the detachment scouted. When they returned, you were absent, and I was alarmed. We searched the mountains for days but then we got word that you had been eaten by a lion. Your gun was brought to us as proof, and your horse returned to camp the day after you vanished. Lieutenant Gernois felt awful; he blamed himself. It was he who insisted on personally carrying out the search, and it was he who found the Arab with your gun. He will be delighted to know that you are safe."

"Doubtless," said Tarzan, with a grim smile.

"He is down in the town now, or I would send for him," continued Captain Gerard. "I shall tell him as soon as he returns." As they talked, Tarzan let Gerard think that after getting lost, he had eventually wandered into the encampment of Kadour ben Muhammad.

As soon as was polite, he bade Gerard *adieu* and headed back to his inn, where Kadour ben Muhammad had interesting information for him. There was a report of a black-bearded European who always went disguised as an Arab, and had been nursing a broken wrist. After some time away from Bou Saada, he was now back, and his whereabouts where known. Tarzan thanked the sheik, then headed for the stranger's hiding-place.

He groped through narrow, stinking alleys, then up a rickety stairway to a closed door and a tiny window without glass. Tarzan could just reach the sill, and raised himself slowly until he could peer inside.

The room was well lit, and at a table sat Rokoff and Gernois.

"Rokoff, you are a devil!" Gernois was saying.

"You have hounded me, destroyed my honor. You have driven me to murder, for the blood of that man Tarzan is on my hands. If that other devil Paulvitch did not know my secret, I would kill you here tonight with my bare hands."

Rokoff laughed. "You would not do that, my dear lieutenant," he said. "The moment I am reported dead, dear Alexei will forward proof of your misdeeds to the Minister of War, and will then charge you with my murder. Come, be sensible. Have I not protected your honor as though it were my own?"

Gernois sneered, and spat out a curse.

"Just one more little payment," continued Rokoff, "deliver the secret papers I desire and the final payment, and you have my word of honor that I shall never ask for anything else from you."

"And no wonder," growled Gernois. "You will have already gotten both my last cent and the only valuable military secret I hold. You ought to be paying me for the information instead."

"I am paying you by my silence," retorted Rokoff. "But enough. You have three minutes to decide. If you refuse, I shall send a note to your commandant tonight that will see you sent to Devil's Island."

For a moment Gernois sat with bowed head. At length he arose. He drew two pieces of paper from his blouse—an official document and a check.

"Here," he said hopelessly. "I had them ready,

for I knew that there could be only one outcome."
He held them toward the Russian.

Rokoff's cruel face lighted in wicked gloating.
He seized the bits of paper. "You have done well,
Gernois," he said. "I shall not trouble you again—
unless you happen to accumulate some more
money or information," and he grinned.

"You never shall again, you dog!" hissed
Gernois. "The next time I shall kill you. I nearly
did tonight. For an hour I sat with these two
pieces of paper, trying to decide whether I should
bring them or my loaded revolver. Next time the
choice shall be easier. Do not tempt fate again,
Rokoff."

Gernois rose to leave. Tarzan barely had time
to drop to the landing and hide in the shadows on
the far side of the doorway, and even then his
cover was weak—he was barely a foot from the
door. Almost immediately it opened, and Gernois
stepped out, Rokoff behind him. Neither spoke.

Gernois had taken perhaps three steps down
the stairway when he halted and half turned, as
though to return. Tarzan expected to be revealed
to Rokoff, who was looking in the opposite direction. Then the officer reconsidered, and continued
downward. Tarzan could hear Rokoff's sigh of
relief. A moment later the Russian went back into
the room and closed the door.

Tarzan gave Gernois time to get well out of
hearing, then pushed open the door and stepped

into the room. Rokoff was reading Gernois' document, and Tarzan was on him before he could rise. As his eyes fell upon the ape-man's face, his own went livid.

"You!" he gasped.

"Yes, it is I," replied Tarzan.

"What do you want?" whispered Rokoff in terror. "Have you come to kill me? You would not dare. They would guillotine you."

"I dare kill you, Rokoff," replied Tarzan, "for no one knows that we are here, and Paulvitch would blame it on Gernois, as you said. But I would not care, Rokoff. Killing you would be such a pleasure that it would be worth any punishment. You are the most despicable coward I have ever heard of, and you deserve death." Tarzan advanced on him.

Rokoff's nerves broke. With a shriek he sprang toward an adjoining room, but the ape-man was on his back in mid-flight. Iron fingers sought his throat and the coward squealed like a stuck pig until Tarzan had shut off his wind. Then the ape-man dragged him to his feet, still choking him. The Russian struggled helplessly in the mighty grasp of Tarzan of the Apes.

Tarzan sat him in a chair, and long before Rokoff would have died, he released his grip. When the Russian's coughing spell was over, Tarzan spoke again.

"That was a taste of death," he said. "But I am

sparing you—this once—solely for the sake of a very good woman who unfortunately had the same mother as you. Should you ever annoy her, her husband or me again—or should you ever return to any French territory—I shall be sure to hunt you down and finish strangling you." Then he turned to the table, on which the two pieces of paper still lay. As he picked them up Rokoff gasped in horror.

Tarzan examined both. He was amazed at what he read. Rokoff had partially read it, but Tarzan knew that no one could remember the facts and figures in it, which were what made it valuable to an enemy of France.

"These will interest the chief of staff," he said, as he slipped them into his pocket. Rokoff groaned. He did not dare curse aloud.

The next morning Tarzan rode north toward Bouira and Algiers. On his route past the hotel, he saw Lieutenant Gernois standing on the porch. When he saw Tarzan he went white as chalk. The ape-man would rather not have seen him, but there he was, so he saluted Gernois as he rode past. Mechanically the lieutenant returned the salute, but his eyes remained wide in horror, like those of a dead man looking on a ghost.

Later, when he reached Sidi Aïssa, Tarzan saw a French officer he had met there on his last visit.

"You left Bou Saada early?" questioned the officer. "Then you have not heard about poor Gernois."

"He was the last man I saw as I rode away," replied Tarzan. "What about him?"

"He is dead. He shot himself about eight o'clock this morning."

Two days later Tarzan reached Algiers. There he found that he would have to wait two more days to catch a ship for Cape Town, so he spent his time writing a full report of his mission. He did not enclose the secret papers, for he dared not let them out of his possession without orders.

After a tedious couple of days, Tarzan boarded his ship. Two fashionably-dressed, smooth-shaven men watched him from an upper deck. The taller had sandy hair and black eyebrows. Later that day they chanced to meet Tarzan on deck, but they quickly looked out to sea, and he did not notice them.

Following the general's instructions, Tarzan had bought his ticket under an assumed name—John Caldwell, London. He wondered at the reason for this order—and at what role he was to play in Cape Town.

At dinner that night Tarzan sat next to a young woman whose place was at the captain's left. The officer introduced her as Miss Strong.

Where had he heard the name before? It sounded familiar. And then the girl's mother gave him the answer, for she addressed her daughter as 'Hazel.'

Hazel Strong! What memories the name inspired. A letter to this girl, penned by the fair hand of Jane Porter, had brought him the first message from the woman he loved. How vividly he recalled the night he had stolen it from the cabin, where Jane Porter had stayed up late writing it. How terrified she would have been if she had known that he was watching her every move.

And this was Hazel Strong—Jane Porter's best friend!

CHAPTER 12

Ships That Pass

Let us go back a few months: our little party of six friends stand on the railway platform in northern Wisconsin. The smoke of forest fires hangs low over the surrounding landscape; its acrid fumes sting their eyes as they stand awaiting the southbound train.

Tarzan has just confessed his love for Jane Porter, but she is determined to keep her promise to William Cecil Clayton, Lord Greystoke. Knowing that he, himself, is the rightful Lord Greystoke, Tarzan keeps that fact secret. Professor Porter wanders off from time to time, always reeled in by Mr. Samuel T. Philander. The faithful Esmeralda, Jane's motherly black helper, is excited to be going home to Maryland. The conversation between Clayton, Jane and Tarzan is strained—and for the latter two, tinged with sadness.

The train announced its approach through the fog of smoke, and the men began to gather up the baggage. Suddenly Clayton exclaimed, "By Jove! I've left my overcoat in the waiting-room," and hastened back inside.

"Goodbye, Jane," said Tarzan, extending his hand. "God bless you!"

"Goodbye," replied the girl faintly. "Try to forget me . . . no, don't. I could not bear it."

"There is no danger of that, dear, though I wish that I could," he answered. "It would be so much easier. You will be happy, though, I am sure. Please tell the others I have decided to drive my car on to New York. I wish to remember Clayton kindly, and as he stands between me and the one person in the world I want, I do not trust myself to bid him a civil good-bye."

Inside, as Clayton bent to pick up his coat, he spotted a telegraph sheet lying face down on the floor. He picked it up, thinking it might be an important message someone had dropped. He glanced at it hastily, and then suddenly he forgot his coat, the approaching train—everything but that terrible little piece of yellow paper in his hand. He read it twice before he could fully grasp what it meant for him.

Before picking it up he had been a proud, wealthy English nobleman. Now he was an untitled and penniless beggar. It was D'Arnot's cablegram to Tarzan, and it read:

Fingerprints prove you Greystoke.
Congratulations.
D'ARNOT

He staggered as though he had received a mortal blow. Just then he heard the others calling to him to hurry—the train was coming to a stop. In a daze he gathered up his overcoat. He would tell them about the cablegram aboard the train. He ran out upon the platform just as the train was preparing to rumble forward, and managed to get aboard; it took a few minutes before the party were settled in their seats. Only then did Clayton learn that Tarzan was gone.

"Where is Tarzan?" he asked Jane Porter. "In another car?"

"No," she replied; "at the last minute he decided to drive his automobile back to New York. He is anxious to see more of America before he returns to France."

Clayton did not reply. How could he explain the cablegram to Jane Porter? Would she still wish to be just plain Mrs. Clayton? Would Tarzan claim his rights? The ape-man had obviously known of the message before he calmly stated that his mother was the ape, Kala. Had he done that for the love of Jane Porter?

No other explanation seemed reasonable. And if that was the case, perhaps he had no plans to ever claim his birthright? And if so, what right had William Cecil Clayton to stand in the way of Tarzan's self-sacrifice? If Tarzan of the Apes wished to save Jane Porter from a future of poverty, how could Clayton jeopardize that future?

And so he kept rationalizing, until his first generous impulse—to surrender his titles and estates to their rightful owner—was fully buried under a mass of excuses. But for the rest of the trip, and for many days afterward, he was moody. He worried that one day Tarzan might regret his unselfishness, and come to claim his rights.

Several days after they reached Baltimore, Clayton suggested to Jane the possibility of early marriage.

"What do you mean by 'early?'" she asked.

"Within the next few days. I must return to England at once, and I want you to return with me, my dear fiancée."

"I can't get ready so soon," replied Jane. "It will take at least a whole month." She was glad for the wedding to be delayed, though she still intended to keep her promise to the bitter end.

"Very well, Jane," he said. "I am disappointed, but I shall delay my trip to England a month and then we can go back together."

But as the month drew to a close, she found still another excuse to postpone. At last, a discouraged Clayton was forced to go back to England alone.

They exchanged letters, but a marriage date came no nearer to being set. Finally, Clayton wrote directly to Professor Porter for support. The old man had always favored the match, and was a conservative Southerner from an old family. He valued titles more than his daughter did. Clayton invited the professor's entire family to be his guests in

London, including Mr. Philander and Esmeralda. Perhaps when Jane was away from ties of home, she would find it easier to take the next step. The evening that he received Clayton's letter, Professor Porter announced that they would leave for London the following week.

But once in London, Jane proved no more eager than she had been in Baltimore—she kept making excuses. When Lord Tennington invited the party to cruise around Africa on his yacht, the *Lady Alice*, she expressed great delight—but absolutely refused to be married until they got back to London. The cruise would take at least a year, with various stops at points of interest. Clayton swore inwardly at the good-hearted Tennington for ever suggesting such a ridiculous trip.

And so it happened that on a certain day, two vessels passed in the Strait of Gibraltar. The smaller, a trim white yacht, was speeding east toward the Suez Canal. On her deck, a young woman idly fingered a diamond-studded locket. Her thoughts and her heart were far away in a jungle.

Upon the deck of the larger vessel, a passenger steamer passing toward the west, a tall, strong man and another young woman idly wondered at the identity of the graceful little yacht. When it had passed, the man resumed their conversation about the United States.

"Yes," he said, "I like America very much, because I like its people, and a country is only

what its people make it. I met some very delightful people there. I recall one family from your own
city, Miss Strong, whom I liked particularly—
Professor Porter and his daughter."

"Jane Porter!" exclaimed the girl. "Why, she is
the very best friend I have in the world. We grew
up together, and are as dear as sisters. I am almost
heartbroken now that I am going to lose her."

"Going to lose her?" exclaimed Tarzan. "Oh,
yes, I understand. You mean that now that she is
married and living in England, you will seldom if
ever see her."

"Yes," she replied, "and what is saddest, she is
not marrying the man she loves! I think it is wicked
to marry out of a sense of duty, and I told her so. I
felt so strongly that I asked her not to invite me to
the wedding, for I could not witness such a mock-
ery. But Jane is positive, and her sense of personal
honor is powerful. Nothing can prevent her from

marrying Lord Greystoke except Greystoke himself—or death."

"I am sorry for her," said Tarzan.

"And I am sorry for the man she loves," said the girl, "for he loves her. I never met him, but from Jane's description, he must be a very wonderful person. It seems that he was born in an African jungle, and raised by fierce apes. He had never seen a white person until Professor Porter and his party were marooned on the coast right at the door of his tiny cabin. He saved them from all manner of terrible beasts, and performed the most amazing feats. Then he and Jane fell in love, though she never really knew it for sure until she had promised herself to Lord Greystoke."

"Most remarkable," murmured Tarzan, anxious to change the subject. Fortunately for him, the girl's mother soon joined them, and the talk became general.

The next few days passed uneventfully, with quiet seas and clear sky. Tarzan spent much time with Miss Strong and her mother, reading, talking, and taking pictures with Miss Strong's camera. After sunset they took walks.

One day Tarzan found Miss Strong in conversation with a strange man he had not seen on board before. As he approached the couple, the man bowed to her and turned to walk away.

"Wait, Monsieur Thuran," said Miss Strong; "you must meet Mr. Caldwell."

The two men shook hands. Monsieur Thuran's eyes were strangely familiar to Tarzan.

"I have had the honor of meeting Monsieur in the past, I am sure," said Tarzan, "though I cannot recall the circumstances."

'Monsieur Thuran' appeared ill at ease. "I cannot say, Monsieur," he replied. "Perhaps."

"Monsieur Thuran has been explaining some of the mysteries of navigation to me," explained Hazel.

Tarzan paid little heed to the following conversation; he was trying to recall where he had met Monsieur Thuran before. Then the sun reached them, and Miss Strong asked Thuran to move her chair farther back into the shade. He did so awkwardly, and Tarzan observed that he had a stiff left wrist and winced briefly in pain. It was the only clue he needed.

Monsieur Thuran had been trying to find an excuse to make a graceful exit, and a lull in the conversation allowed him to do so. Bowing low to Miss Strong, and inclining his head to Tarzan, he turned to leave them.

"Just a moment," said Tarzan. "If Miss Strong will pardon me, I will accompany you. I shall return in a moment, Miss Strong."

Monsieur Thuran looked uncomfortable. When the two men had passed out of the girl's sight, Tarzan stopped, laying a heavy hand on the other's shoulder.

"What is your game now, Rokoff?" he asked.

"I am leaving France as I promised you," replied Rokoff, resentfully.

"I see you are," said Tarzan, "but I know you too well to believe that your presence on this boat is just a coincidence, especially as you are in disguise."

"Well," growled Rokoff, with a shrug, "You can do nothing about it. This vessel flies the English flag. I have as much right on board her as you, and from the fact that you are booked under a false name, perhaps I have even more right."

"We will not discuss it, Rokoff. All I want to tell you is this: Miss Strong is too decent a woman for your kind. Stay away from her."

Rokoff turned scarlet.

"If you don't, I shall throw you overboard," continued Tarzan. "I am just waiting for some excuse." Then he turned on his heel and left Rokoff standing there, trembling with suppressed rage.

He did not see the man again for days, but Rokoff was not idle. In his stateroom with Paulvitch he fumed, swore, and threatened terrible revenge.

"I would throw him overboard tonight," he cried, "were I sure he was not carrying those papers. I cannot chance pitching them into the ocean with him. If you were not such a stupid coward, Alexei, you would find a way to enter his stateroom and search for the documents."

Paulvitch smiled. "You are supposed to be the brains of this partnership, my dear Nikolai," he replied. "Why do you not figure out a way?"

Two hours later they got lucky. Paulvitch was keeping watch on Tarzan, and saw him leave his room without locking the door. Five minutes later Rokoff was keeping watch while Paulvitch sifted through the ape-man's luggage. He was about to give up when he saw Tarzan's coat hanging up. He searched it and found an official envelope, and a quick glance at its contents brought a broad smile to the Russian's face.

As a professional burglar, Paulvitch made sure to leave the stateroom looking exactly as it had been before. When he handed the packet to Rokoff back in their stateroom, the larger man rang for a steward and ordered champagne to celebrate.

"It was luck, Nikolai," explained Paulvitch. "Clearly he usually keeps these papers on his person at all times, but this time he slipped up. But when he finds out, he will suspect you immediately."

"It will make no difference who he suspects—after tonight," said Rokoff with an evil grin.

That night Tarzan stood leaning over the rail looking far out to sea, as he did every night for an hour. Watching eyes, of course, had noted this habit—and they watched him now.

Presently the last straggler had left the deck. The night was starry but moonless.

From the shadows, two figures crept stealthily up on the ape-man from behind. The background noises of waves, propeller and engines drowned out what little sound they made.

They were quite close to him now, crouching low, like football players. One of them raised his hand and lowered it, as though counting off seconds—one—two—three! In unison the two leaped for their victim. Each grasped a leg, and before Tarzan of the Apes could turn to save himself, he was plummeting toward the Atlantic.

Hazel Strong was watching out her porthole window across the sea. Suddenly a body shot past her eyes from the deck above. It dropped so quickly into the dark waters below that she could not be sure what it was—it might have been a man. She listened for some outcry from above: "Man overboard!" but it did not come. All was silence.

The girl decided that it must have been a bundle of refuse thrown overboard by a deckhand, and went to bed.

CHAPTER 13

The Wreck of the *Lady Alice*

The next morning at breakfast, to Miss Strong's mild surprise, Tarzan's place was vacant. As she was sitting on deck later, Monsieur Thuran paused to chat with her for the first time in awhile. He seemed most cheerful and charming.

The day dragged. She missed the quiet companionship of Mr. Caldwell, whom she had liked from the first—especially his wise and entertaining way of describing the places, peoples and animals he had seen. When Monsieur Thuran stopped to talk with her again later that day, she welcomed the company but had grown quite concerned by Mr. Caldwell's continued absence. She feared that it had to do with the object falling past her window the night before. Finally she raised the subject:

"Monsieur Thuran, have you seen Mr. Caldwell today?"

"No. Why do you ask?" he replied.

"I have not seen him since yesterday," explained Hazel.

Monsieur Thuran replied with silky courtesy.

"I did not know Mr. Caldwell well," he said. "He seemed a fine gentleman, however. Perhaps he is not feeling well—seasickness perhaps—and has remained in his stateroom? It would not be strange."

"No," replied the girl, "it would not. But for some reason, I have a feeling that all is not well with Mr. Caldwell. It seems almost as though he is no longer aboard the ship."

Monsieur Thuran laughed pleasantly. "My dear Miss Strong, where else could he be? We have not sighted land for days."

"Of course, it is ridiculous of me," she admitted. "But I am tired of worrying about it. I am going to find out where he is." She motioned to a passing steward.

"That may be more difficult than you imagine, my dear girl," thought Monsieur Thuran, but aloud he said: "By all means."

"Find Mr. Caldwell, please," she said to the steward, "and tell him that his friends are worried by his absence."

"You are very fond of Mr. Caldwell?" asked Monsieur Thuran.

"I think he is splendid," replied the girl. "And mamma adores him. He makes a woman feel safe and confident."

Shortly the steward returned to report that Mr. Caldwell was not in his stateroom. "I cannot find him, Miss Strong, and"—he hesitated—"his bed was not occupied last night. I must report it to the captain."

"Most assuredly," exclaimed Miss Strong. "I shall go with you to the captain myself. I just know that something awful has happened!"

They met with the captain a few moments later. Their stories caused him concern. The steward had searched the vessel high and low for the passenger, he said.

"And are you sure, Miss Strong, that you saw a body fall overboard last night?" he asked.

"I think so," she answered. "I cannot say that it was a human body—there was no outcry. It might have been only a bundle of trash, as I had thought. But if Mr. Caldwell is not found, I shall be sure it was he whom I saw fall past my porthole."

The captain ordered a thorough search of the entire ship while Miss Strong remained in his cabin, to await the outcome. Responding to the captain's questions about the missing man, she realized how little, indeed, Mr. Caldwell had told her about his past. He said he had been born in Africa and educated in Paris. Even that had only come out when she remarked upon the oddity of an Englishman having such a heavy French accent.

"Did he ever speak of any enemies?" asked the captain.

"Never."

"Was he acquainted with any of the other passengers?"

"Only casually, as he had been with me."

"Er—in your opinion, Miss Strong, did he drink to excess?"

"I do not know that he drank at all. He certainly had not been drinking that evening," she answered, "not while I was with him."

"It is very strange," said the captain. "He did not look to me like the sort of man who would faint. And even if he had fainted, he would have tended to fall toward the deck, not overboard. If he is not on board, Miss Strong, he was thrown overboard. No one heard an outcry, which would suggest that he was dead before he left the ship's deck. Murdered."

The girl shuddered.

A full hour later, the first officer returned to report on the search. "Mr. Caldwell is not on board, sir," he said.

"I fear that there is something very sinister here, Mr. Brently," said the captain. "Search carefully through Mr. Caldwell's effects, to see if there would be a motive for either suicide or murder. Let us get to the bottom of this."

"Aye, aye, sir!" responded Brently, and left.

Hazel Strong remained in her cabin for two days, and when she finally ventured on deck she looked pale and tired. Waking or sleeping, all she could see was that dark body dropping silently into the cold, grim sea. Shortly after her first reappearance on deck, Monsieur Thuran joined her to express his sympathy.

"It is terrible, Miss Strong," he said. "I cannot rid my mind of it."

"Nor I," said the girl wearily. "I feel that he might have been saved had I said something."

"You must not blame yourself for what is not your fault, my dear Miss Strong," urged Monsieur Thuran. "Who would assume that some object falling into the sea from a ship must surely be a man? Had you given the alarm, at first they would have doubted your story as a nervous fantasy. Even then, had you insisted, they would have had to halt the ship, lower boats, and row them back in search of an unknown spot. By then it would have been too late and the result would be the same. You have done more than any of us for poor Mr. Caldwell—you initiated the search."

The girl appreciated his reassurances. He was with her almost constantly for the remainder of the voyage, and she grew to like him very much. Monsieur Thuran had learned that the beautiful Miss Strong, was an American heiress—wealthy in her own right, and with excellent future prospects.

Monsieur Thuran had meant to leave the ship soon after getting rid of Tarzan, then return to Russia with his prize—but now he had another idea. That American fortune—and its heiress— were tempting. She would cause quite a sensation in St. Petersburg, and so would he, with the help of her inheritance. The more he considered it, the better it sounded.

He suddenly decided that important business required him to make a long stay in Cape Town. Miss Strong had told him that she and her mother were to visit Hazel's uncle there, and would probably stay for some months. To her delight, Monsieur Thuran said he would also be there.

"I hope that we shall be able to see one another," she said. "You must call upon mamma and me as soon as we are settled."

"I would be delighted to do so," he said immediately.

Mrs. Strong was not quite as impressed by him as her daughter. "I do not know why I distrust him," she said to Hazel one day. "He seems like a perfect gentleman, but sometimes his eyes give me an odd feeling."

The girl laughed. "You are a silly dear, mamma," she said.

"I suppose so, but I would rather we had poor Mr. Caldwell for company instead."

"And I, too," replied her daughter.

Monsieur Thuran became a frequent visitor at the home of Hazel Strong's uncle in Cape Town. He seemed to show up any time they wanted or needed something. The ladies soon grew to depend upon him, and her uncle and his family grew to appreciate his tireless courtesy and service very much.

At last, when the moment seemed right, he proposed marriage to her. Miss Strong was startled. She did not know what to say.

"I had never thought that you loved me," she told him. "You have become a very dear friend, but I have never thought that I loved you. Let us continue to be friends, while I consider my feelings from a different angle. Perhaps I will find that I feel more than friendship."

"Absolutely, Miss Strong. I deeply regret my haste, but I have loved you from the first time I saw you, and thought it was clear to everyone. I am willing to wait, for I am certain that a love as great and pure as mine will be rewarded. I ask only this: do you love another?"

"I have never been in love in my life," she replied, and he was quite satisfied.

On the way home that night he pictured himself buying a steam yacht, and building a costly villa on the sunny shores of the Black Sea.

The next day Hazel Strong enjoyed one of the happiest surprises of her life: she met Jane Porter, of all people, coming out of a jeweler's shop! "Why, Jane Porter!" she exclaimed. "Where in the world did you come from? Why, I can't believe my own eyes."

"Well, of all things!" cried the equally astonished Jane. "And here I have been imagining you back in Baltimore!" They embraced warmly.

Mutual explanations were made, and Hazel learned that Lord Tennington's yacht, *Lady Alice*, was in Cape Town for at least a week, after which she would continue up the West African coast—then back to England. "Where," Jane concluded, "I am to be married."

"Then you are not married yet?" asked Hazel.

"Not yet," replied Jane, and then, "I wish England were a million miles away."

The yachting party and Hazel's relatives began to socialize. Each hosted dinners, and the visitors were taken on a trip through the country. Monsieur Thuran was a welcome guest at every function. He gave a dinner for the men of the party, and managed to gain favor with Lord Tennington by many little acts of hospitality. Once when he was alone with Lord Tennington, he mentioned that his engagement to Miss Strong was to be announced immediately upon their return to America. "But not a word of it, my dear Tennington—not a word of it."

"Certainly, I quite understand, my dear fellow," Tennington had replied. "But you are to be congratulated—she really is a wonderful girl."

The next day, Mrs. Strong, Hazel, and Monsieur Thuran were guests aboard Lord Tennington's yacht. Mrs. Strong had been telling them how much she had enjoyed her visit at Cape Town, but a letter just received from her lawyers back in Baltimore required her to cut short her visit.

"When do you sail?" asked Tennington.

"The first of the week, I think," she replied.

"Indeed?" exclaimed Monsieur Thuran. "I am

very fortunate. I, too, have found that I must return at once, and now I shall have the honor of accompanying and serving you."

"That is nice of you, Monsieur Thuran," replied Mrs. Strong. "We shall be glad for your company." But for reasons she could not pinpoint, she would rather he was not coming.

"By Jove!" exclaimed Lord Tennington a moment later. "I have a wonderful idea!"

"Yes, Tennington, of course," said Clayton peevishly. "Any idea of yours must surely be a grand idea. Are we going to steam to China via the South Pole?"

"Oh, I say now, Clayton," returned Tennington, "you needn't be so grumpy. You're just miffed that you didn't suggest the trip yourself, and you have been a wet blanket ever since we sailed. No, sir," he continued, "you will all like this idea. Let us take Mrs. and Miss Strong, and Thuran, too, if he'll come, as far as England with us on the yacht. Now, won't that be grand?"

"Forgive me, Tenny, old boy," cried Clayton. "It certainly *is* a grand idea—I never would have suspected you of it. You're quite sure it's your own?"

"And we'll sail the first of the week, or any other time that suits you, Mrs. Strong," concluded the big-hearted Englishman, as though the matter were agreed.

"Mercy, Lord Tennington, you haven't even given us an opportunity to thank you, much less decide whether we can accept," said Mrs. Strong.

"Why, of course you'll come," responded Tennington. "We'll make as good time as any passenger boat, and you'll be just as comfortable. Anyway, we all want you, and won't take no for an answer." And so it was settled that they would sail the following Monday.

Two days out of Cape Town the girls were sitting in Hazel's cabin aboard the *Lady Alice*, looking at some photos she had gotten developed. They were the story of her travels since leaving America, and Jane had many questions about the people and scenes Hazel had encountered.

"And here," she said suddenly, "here's a man you know! Poor fellow, I have so often meant to ask you about him, but it always slipped my mind." Jane did not see the face of the man the little photo portrayed. "His name was John Caldwell, an Englishman," continued Hazel. "Do you recall him? He said that he met you in America."

"I do not recollect the name," replied Jane. "Let me see the picture."

"The poor fellow was lost overboard on our trip down the coast," she said, as she handed the print to Jane.

"Lost over—Why, Hazel, Hazel—don't tell me that he is drowned at sea! Hazel! Please say that you are joking!" And Jane Porter began to quietly weep.

Hazel held her friend, and sat looking at her for a long time before either spoke.

"I did not know, Jane," said Hazel carefully, "that you knew Mr. Caldwell so well that his death could shock you so."

"'John Caldwell?'" questioned Miss Porter. "You mean to tell me that you do not know who this man was, Hazel?"

"Why, of course I do. His name was John Caldwell; he was from London."

"Oh, Hazel, I wish I could believe it," moaned Jane. "But those features are burned so deep into my memory and my heart that I would recognize them anywhere."

"What do you mean, Jane?" cried Hazel, now thoroughly alarmed. "Who do you think it is?"

"I don't think, Hazel, *I know*. This is a picture of Tarzan of the Apes."

"Jane!"

"I cannot be mistaken. Oh, Hazel, are you sure that he is dead?"

"I am afraid so, dear," answered Hazel sadly. "I wish he were not, but it is all coming back to me now. He said that he had been born in Africa, and educated in France."

"Yes, that would be true," murmured Jane Porter dully.

"The first officer searched his luggage, but found nothing to identify John Caldwell, of London. Practically all his belongings were made or bought in Paris. Everything that bore an initial was marked either with a 'T' alone, or with 'J.C. T.' We thought that he was traveling incognito under his first two names—the J.C. standing for John Caldwell."

"Tarzan of the Apes took the name Jean C. Tarzan," said Jane lifelessly. "And he is dead! Oh, Hazel, it is horrible! He died all alone in this terrible ocean! He was full of life, health and strength, and now he is the prey of slimy, crawling things . . ." With a little moan she buried her head in her arms, and sank sobbing to the floor.

For days Miss Porter was ill, and would see no one except Hazel and the kindly Esmeralda. When at last she came on deck all were struck by the sad change in her. She was but a mournful shell of the alert, charming American beauty who had delighted everyone previously. The entire party strove to cheer and amuse her, but all to no avail. Occasionally the jolly Tennington would wring a faint smile from her, but for the most part she sat looking wide-eyed out across the sea.

With Jane Porter's illness one misfortune after another seemed to attack the yacht. First an engine broke down, and they drifted for two days while repairs were made. Then a sudden squall washed overboard nearly everything on deck that was not tied down. Later two of the seamen got into a fight—one was badly knifed, and the other clapped in irons. Worst of all, the first mate fell overboard at night, and drowned before help could reach him.

The entire ship's company was depressed by the bad luck. The sailors now recalled all sorts of terrible omens and warnings earlier in the voyage, and all were sure that worse tragedies were to come. They did not have long to wait.

The second night after the mate's drowning, about one o'clock in the morning, a terrific impact threw the slumbering guests and crew from bed and bunk. A mighty shudder heeled the craft far over to starboard—she hung there for a moment, then with a great tearing sound, she slipped back upright.

Instantly the men rushed out onto the deck, followed closely by the women. The night was cloudy, but the sea was calm, and just off the port bow a black object could be seen low in the water. "A derelict," explained of the officer of the watch.

Presently the engineer hurried on deck in search of the captain. "That patch we put on the cylinder head's blown out, sir," he reported, "and she's takin' water fast."

An instant later a seaman rushed up from below. "My Gawd!" he cried. "Her whole bleedin' bottom's ripped out. She can't float twenty minutes."

"Shut up!" roared Tennington. "Ladies, go below and get some of your things together at once, please, just in case we have to take to the boats. Captain Jerrold, please send some competent man below to evaluate the damage. In the meantime, I might suggest that you ready the boats."

The calm, low voice of the owner tended to reassure the entire party, and a moment later all were obeying him. By the time the ladies had returned to the deck, the boats were nearly ready. The officer who had been sent below returned to give his report.

"Well, sir?" said the captain.

The officer hesitated. "I dislike frightening the ladies, sir," he said, "but she can't float a dozen minutes, in my opinion. There's a hole in her you could drive a milk cow through, sir."

For five minutes the *Lady Alice* had been settling lower in the water toward the bow. Already her stern loomed high in the air, making it difficult to stand on deck. Her four boats were all filled and lowered away in safety.

As they pulled rapidly from the stricken vessel Jane Porter turned for one last look at her. Just then there came a loud crash, then a great rumbling and pounding from the heart of the ship. Some great machinery had come loose, and was smashing through bulkheads toward the sinking bow. The stern rose high above them, seemed to pause for a moment when nearly vertical, and the doomed *Lady Alice* slipped swiftly beneath the waves.

The brave Lord Tennington wiped a tear from his eye as he sat in one of the small boats. It was not a fortune he saw sinking forever into the sea, but a dear, beautiful friend that he had loved.

At last the long night ended, and a tropical sun shone down upon the rolling water. Jane Porter awakened from a fitful slumber to see three sailors, Clayton, and Monsieur Thuran in the boat with her. Then she looked for the other boats, but there was nothing to break the fearful monotony of that watery waste. They were alone in a small boat upon the broad Atlantic.

CHAPTER 14

Back to the Primitive

As Tarzan struck the water, he first swam clear of the ship's dangerous propellers. He tread water for a time, disgusted that Rokoff had so easily bested him. He never thought to call for help, as he watched the receding lights of the steamer fade away—he had never done that in all his life.

There was a tiny chance that he might be picked up, he thought, and an even smaller chance that he would reach land. To combine these chances, he would swim slowly toward the coast—maybe the ship had not been far from shore. He swam with long, easy strokes, conserving his awesome strength. Clothing weighed him down, and first his shoes and then his trousers went. He would have removed his coat, but for the precious papers in it. He felt to assure himself that they were still there—they were not!

Now he knew that Rokoff had acted on more than revenge: the Russian had gotten back the papers Tarzan had wrested from him at Bou Saada. The ape-man swore softly, and discarded the rest of his clothes. He swam unhindered, guided by the stars, ever eastward.

The first faint evidence of dawn was breaking ahead of him when a low-lying black mass loomed up directly ahead. A few strong strokes brought him to the side of a wave-washed, overturned derelict ship. Tarzan clambered onto it to rest at least until daylight; then he would continue on. Better to die trying to save himself than to remain and perish of hunger and thirst. The sea was quiet, and he had not slept in twenty hours. Soon Tarzan of the Apes was fast asleep upon the slimy timbers.

The heat of the sun awoke him early. He was terribly thirsty, and growing more so. A moment later, two discoveries made him forget his discomfort. The first was a mass of wreckage floating alongside, in the midst of which bobbed a capsized lifeboat. The second was a dim, distant shoreline on the horizon to the east.

Tarzan dove into the water, and swam to the lifeboat. The cool ocean refreshed him, and soon he succeeded in hauling the lifeboat up onto the overturned hulk. It was in good shape, and he soon had it in the water right side up. With a couple of sturdier pieces of wreckage as paddles, he headed for that far-off shore.

It was late in the afternoon by the time he could make out details on the coast. Before him lay a little, landlocked harbor. The wooded point to the north was strangely familiar. Could fate have washed him up at the very edge of his own beloved jungle? As he entered the harbor, doubt vanished—for there, in the shadow of his forest, stood the cabin built by his long-dead father: John Clayton, Lord Greystoke.

Energized with joy, with long powerful strokes Tarzan sent the little craft speeding toward the beach. He leaped to shore; his heart beat faster as each long-familiar object came into view. There were the cabin, the beach, the little brook, the dense jungle. He saw the many birds in their brilliant plumage and the gorgeous tropical blooms hanging on vines from the giant trees.

Tarzan of the Apes was home.

He announced his return immediately: he threw back his head and gave the fierce, wild challenge of his tribe. For a moment silence reigned upon the jungle, and then came a low answering challenge—it was the deep roar of Numa, the lion. And then, faintly, and from a great distance, came the fearsome answering bellow of a bull ape.

First, Tarzan went to the brook to quench his thirst. Then he approached his cabin, and found the door still latched shut as he and D'Arnot had left it. He entered. Nothing had been disturbed. There were the table, the bed, and the little crib built by his father—the shelves and cupboards just as he had left them nearly two years before.

His eyes and thirst satisfied, it was time to do the same for his stomach. There was nothing in the cabin, nor had he any weapons; but on a wall hung one of his old grass ropes, one often broken and spliced. Tarzan wished that he had a knife, a spear, and a bow and arrows. He would attend to that before sunset, but in the meantime, the rope would get him some food. He threw it over his shoulder, closed the door behind him and headed for the jungle.

Tarzan of the Apes plunged into the dense woodland, wary and noiseless, once more a savage beast hunting its food. For a time he kept to the ground, but finding no trail of prey, he took to the trees. With the first dizzy swing all the old joy of living swept over him. Vain regrets and dull heartache were forgotten. Now, indeed, he had the true happiness of perfect freedom. Who would go back to the stifling, wicked cities when the mighty reaches of the great jungle offered peace and liberty? Not he.

While it was still light out, Tarzan came to a clear spot at a ford in the river, where he knew the beasts of the jungle would come down to drink. Here, on many nights, one might find Sabor or Numa crouching in the dense foliage, hoping to surprise Bara, the deer, or Horta, the boar. Here, now, came Tarzan of the Apes to do the same.

On a low branch he squatted above the trail. He waited for an hour as it grew dark. A little to one side of the ford he heard the faint sound of padded feet, and the brushing of a huge body against tall grasses. The ape-man knew that sound well: Numa, the lion, and on the same errand. Tarzan smiled.

Presently he heard, and then saw, Horta approaching the watering-hole. Here was delicious meat—and Tarzan's mouth watered. Numa now lay ominously still. The wild pig passed beneath Tarzan—a few more steps and he would be within range of Numa's spring. Tarzan could imagine Numa already sucking in his breath for the awful roar which would freeze his prey for the brief instant before his terrible fangs would splinter Horta's bones.

But as Numa inhaled, a slender rope flew from the low branches of a nearby tree, and its noose settled around Horta's neck. There was a frightened grunt, a squeal, and then Numa's quarry was dragged backward up the trail. As he sprang, his dinner soared upward beyond his clutches into the tree above, and a mocking face looked down at him and laughed.

Then indeed did Numa roar. Infuriated and hungry, he paced back and forth beneath the taunting ape-man. Now he stopped, rose on his hind legs and sharpened his huge claws in rage upon the bark of Tarzan's tree, laying bare the white wood beneath.

In the meantime Tarzan had dragged the struggling Horta to the limb beside him. Strong fingers completed the work of the choking noose.

The ape-man had no knife, but he had sharp teeth, and they soon tore into the delicious meat while the raging lion watched someone else eat his meal. Stray fallen droplets of Horta's flesh and blood only served to taunt and enrage Numa further, and he gave full vent to his fury.

It was quite dark by the time Tarzan had eaten his fill. How superior this was to the ruined, scorched flesh served to him by civilized men. He had never gotten used to it. Always he had craved the warm, bloody meat of the fresh kill.

He wiped his hands on some leaves, slung the rest of Horta across his shoulder, and swung off through the jungle toward his cabin. At the same instant, in the Indian Ocean on the far side of Africa, Jane Porter and William Cecil Clayton arose from a fine dinner onboard the *Lady Alice*.

Beneath Tarzan walked Numa, the lion, and when the ape-man glanced downward he caught occasional glimpses of the baleful green eyes following through the darkness. Numa now stalked him quietly, a great feline shadow, but Tarzan heard his every step. Tarzan hoped he would not stalk him to his cabin door, for that would mean a night's sleep curled in the fork of a tree rather than in his comfortable cabin. But, after a while, Numa gave up the chase and, with a final salvo of enraged roars, turned angrily back in search of an easier dinner. So Tarzan came to his cabin alone, and a few moments later was curled up in the mildewed remnants of what had once been a grassy bed.

And so Monsieur Jean C. Tarzan shed the thin skin of civilization, and sank happy and contented into the deep sleep of the satisfied wild beast—yet the word "yes" from a woman would have bound him to civilization forever, and made the thought of this savage existence repulsive.

Tarzan slept late the next morning, for the previous day had used muscles that were quite out of shape. When he awoke he first ran to the brook to drink. Then he went for a swim in the sea, after which he returned to his cabin to breakfast off the leftover flesh of Horta. He buried the rest of the carcass in the soft earth outside the cabin, for dinner at some later time.

Once more he took his rope and vanished into the jungle. This time he hunted nobler quarry—man—although in his own opinion many jungle beasts were nobler than man. Today Tarzan sought weapons. He wondered if the women and children had remained in Mbonga's village after the French expedition had avenged D'Arnot's supposed death. If the village were deserted, he would have a long search for another one.

The ape-man traveled swiftly through the forest, and arrived at the village around noon. Unfortunately it was abandoned, with overgrown fields and collapsing huts. He searched the ruins for about half an hour, hoping to find some forgotten weapon, but no luck. Giving up, he hunted and scavenged up the stream, which ran southeast—settlements tended to be sited next to fresh water.

That evening his quick noose brought him another hearty meal thanks to the flesh of Bara, the deer. His travel had now taken him far inland, so he spent the night in the comfy fork of a giant tree a hundred feet above the ground.

Early the next morning he continued upstream. For three days he traveled, until he came to a new part of the jungle. The forest began to thin as the altitude rose, and in the distance he saw mighty mountain ranges overlooking the wide grassy plains of the famed African savanna. Here was new game: antelope and zebra. Tarzan was excited by this visit to a new world.

On the morning of the fourth day his nostrils suddenly caught a faint new scent: man. Tarzan thrilled with pleasure. Every sense was alert as he moved craftily through the trees, upwind, in the direction of his prey. Presently he came upon a lone African warrior treading softly through the jungle.

Tarzan followed close above his quarry, waiting for a clear space in which to hurl his rope, but now he was a different man. Seldom if ever, he recalled, did civilized man kill a fellow man without some good reason. True, Tarzan wanted this man's weapons and ornaments; but need Tarzan kill him to get them? The longer he considered it, the less eager he was to kill the man. While he was trying to decide what to do, they came to a clearing. At the far side lay a palisaded village of beehive-like huts.

As the warrior emerged from the forest, Tarzan briefly spotted a tawny hide worming its way through the thick grasses behind them: Numa was also stalking the black man. Now Tarzan saw the African as a fellow man, threatened by a common enemy.

There was no time to mull it over, for Numa was about to leap. Then a number of things happened almost all at once. Numa pounced; Tarzan cried out a warning; and the warrior whirled just in time to see Numa halted in mid-flight by a slender noose of rope which had fallen cleanly around his neck.

The ape-man had not had time to brace himself for the strain of Numa's mass upon the rope. The noose caused the lion's mighty talons to fall well short of the African's flesh, but the impact pulled Tarzan tumbling to earth less than six paces from the infuriated predator. Like lightning, Numa turned on this new enemy, and Tarzan of the Apes was nearer to death than he had ever been before.

The proud African warrior realized in an instant that he owed his life to this strange white man. It would take a miracle to keep those huge fangs out of his savior's body, but he must try.

Quick as thought, his spear arm went back, and then came forward with all the force of his own powerful muscles. The African's cast was flawless, and the iron-tipped weapon tore through Numa from the right side all the way to the left shoulder.

With a hideous scream of rage and pain the brute whirled upon the black spearman. Numa had gone only a dozen paces when Tarzan's rope halted him once more—then he wheeled again upon the ape-man, only to feel the painful sting of a barbed arrow as it sank deep in his quivering flesh, for the African was as calm and capable with the bow as he was with a spear. The lion turned again, but by this time Tarzan had wrapped the rope a couple of times around the trunk of a great tree, then tied it.

The black warrior saw the trick and grinned fierce approval, but Tarzan knew that Numa must be quickly finished before those mighty teeth found the slender cord that held him. He darted to the African's side and quickly drew the warrior's long knife, then by sign language told him to keep shooting at the great beast while he, Tarzan, closed in with the knife. Nodding his understanding, the tribesman peppered Numa with arrows, keeping the beast raging in one direction while Tarzan snuck up from the other. Numa roared, moaned, shrieked and split the air with rearing leaps in the effort to get at his tormentors.

But at length the agile ape-man saw his

chance, and rushed in on the beast's left side behind the mighty shoulder. A giant arm encircled the tawny throat, and a long blade sank directly into the fierce heart.

Then Tarzan arose, and the black man and the white man looked into each other's eyes across the body of their kill.

The African gave the sign of peace and friendship, and Tarzan of the Apes answered in kind.

CHAPTER 15

From Ape to Tribesman

The noise of their battle had drawn an excited group from the nearby village. A moment after the lion's death, the two men were surrounded by African warriors, all talking and gesturing at once.

And then the women came, and the children, eager and curious—especially at the sight of Tarzan. The ape-man's new friend finally succeeded in relating the story, and soon the villagers were eager to honor the strange creature who had saved their fellow tribesman and fought fierce Numa alongside him.

At last they led him into their village, where they gave him many gifts of food. When he pointed to their weapons, the warriors hastened to fetch spear, shield, arrows, and a bow. His new comrade-in-arms gave him the knife Tarzan had used to kill Numa. The grateful villagers would have given him anything he asked for.

Tarzan thought about how much easier this was than murdering and robbing to get what he wanted. He had been so close to killing this man whom he never had seen before, and who was now showing him honest friendship and generosity. Tarzan of the Apes was ashamed of what he had planned. Hereafter he would kill no man unless he knew the man deserved it.

This brought Rokoff to Tarzan's mind. He wished he could have the Russian to himself in the dark jungle for a few minutes—there was a man who deserved killing if anyone did. And if he could have seen Rokoff at that moment—doing his utmost to slither into Miss Strong's affections—he would have been, if possible, even more ready to sentence the Russian to die.

Tarzan's first night with the tribe was devoted to a wild feast in his honor. The hunters had brought in an antelope and a zebra, and gallons of mild native beer were consumed. As the warriors danced in the firelight, Tarzan was impressed by their handsome features. The men and women alike looked intelligent and dignified.

During this dance the ape-man first noticed that some of the men and many of the women wore golden anklets and heavy armlets. When he gestured a wish to examine one of these, the woman removed it from her arm and insisted, through signs, that Tarzan accept it as a gift. It was indeed of solid gold, and it surprised him, for he had seen few such ornaments among African tribes. He tried to ask them where the metal came from, but could not convey his question.

When the dance was done Tarzan signaled his intention to leave them, but they urged him to accept the hospitality of a large hut set aside by the chief for Tarzan's sole use. He tried to explain that he would return in the morning, but could not make them understand. They watched, mystified, as he walked away toward the side of the village opposite the gate. He preferred to spend the night in the fresh air of the swaying trees.

The natives followed him to where an immense tree overhung the palisade. To their astonishment, Tarzan leaped like Manu, the monkey, into the foliage above. For half an hour they called to him to return, but getting no answer, they went to bed. Tarzan went a short distance into the forest until he found a tree he liked, then curled up in a large fork and fell asleep.

The following morning he dropped into the village as suddenly as he had disappeared the preceding night. For a moment the natives were startled and afraid, but their previous night's guest was soon welcomed with shouts and laughter. That day he joined a party of warriors on a great hunting trip to the nearby plains. The strange white man's hunting skill with their own weapons brought him still more respect from the proud Africans.

For weeks Tarzan lived with his new friends, hunting buffalo, antelope, and zebra for meat, and elephant for ivory. Quickly he learned their speech, their native customs, and their tribal ethics. The warrior he had saved, whose name was Busuli, shared many of the tribal legends and history with Tarzan: how, long ago, his people had come many long marches from the north. They had once been a great and powerful tribe, until Arab slave raiders had attacked them with deadly guns—reducing them to a mere shadow of their former numbers and power.

"They hunted us down like animals," said Busuli. "They showed us no mercy. They sought slaves, or ivory, or both. Our men were killed and our women driven away like sheep. We fought against them for many years, but our arrows and spears could not defeat the sticks that spit fire and death far beyond the reach of our mightiest archer. At last, when my father was a young man, the Arabs came again, but our warriors saw them a long way off. Chowambi, who was chief then, told his people to gather up their belongings and escape with him to the south. They would march until they found a spot where the Arab raiders could not find them.

"They did so, carrying all their belongings, including many tusks of ivory. For months they wandered, suffering great hardship. Much of the way was through dense jungle and across mighty mountains. Finally they came to this spot, and although they sent parties farther on to search for an even better location, none has ever been found."

"And the raiders have never found you here?" asked Tarzan.

"About a year ago a small party of Arabs and their slaves, the Manyuema, our traditional tribal enemies from the north, stumbled upon us, but we drove them off, killing many. For days we followed them, picking them off one by one until only a handful remained, but these escaped us."

As Busuli talked, he fingered a heavy gold armlet that shone brightly against his ebony skin. This made Tarzan recall the question he had tried unsuccessfully to ask before. For weeks he had not thought about the source of these ornaments, but the sleeping greed of civilization was suddenly awakened in him. He pointed to the armlet.

"Where did the yellow metal come from, Busuli?" he asked.

The African pointed southeast. "A moon's march away—maybe more," he replied.

"Have you been there?" asked Tarzan.

"No, but some of our people were there years ago, when my father was yet a young man. When we were searching for a better location, one of the scouting parties, led by Chowambi, came upon a strange people who wore many ornaments of yellow metal. Their spears were tipped with it, as were their arrows, and they cooked in pots made of this metal.

"They lived in a great village of stone huts surrounded by a high wall. They were very fierce, attacking our warriors before learning that they came in peace. Our men were few in number, but they held their own at the top of a little rocky hill. At sunset, the fierce people went back into their wicked city. Then our warriors came down from their hill and took many ornaments of yellow metal from the bodies of those they had slain. They marched back out of the valley, and none of us have ever returned.

"They are wicked people—neither white like you nor black like me, but covered with hair like Bolgani, the gorilla. Yes, they are very bad people indeed, and Chowambi was glad to get out of their country."

"Are any still living who went with Chowambi, and saw these strange people and their city?" asked Tarzan.

"Waziri, our chief, was there," replied Busuli. "He was a very young man then, but he accompanied his father, Chowambi."

So that night, Tarzan asked old Waziri about it. The chief remembered the route well; it was easy to follow, but a long march. He told the story:

"It took us many days. We followed our stream to its source in the mountains, crossed them, and then followed another stream. It went down, then up and led us to another mountain range. We decided to climb these mountains, and if we saw no sign of a better place to settle, we would return. From the summit we saw a valley, and beyond it a village of stone. Much of it had fallen over in decay." From this point, Waziri's story was quite similar to Busuli's.

"I should like to go there and see this strange city," said Tarzan, "and get some of their yellow metal from its fierce people."

"It is a long march," replied Waziri, "and I am an old man, but if you will wait until the rainy season is over and the rivers have receded I will take some of my warriors and go with you."

Tarzan had to accept this, though he felt impatient, and would have liked to set out the next morning.

The next day one member of a small hunting party returned to the village from the south to report a big herd of elephants some miles away. This meant much wealth in the form of ivory. The rest of the day and evening were spent preparing weapons for a great hunt, while the village shaman dispensed various charms and amulets for protection and good fortune.

At dawn the hunters were off, fifty strong. Tarzan's brown skin contrasted oddly with the deep black of his African comrades' flesh; but except for color, he was one of them. He wore their ornaments, wielded their weapons, and spoke their language. He laughed and joked with them, and leaped and shouted in the wild dance prior to their departure. He had far more in common with these people than his Parisian friends, whose ways he had mimicked for a few months.

He thought of D'Arnot, and grinned in amusement as he imagined what the Frenchman would say if he were here now. Poor Paul, who felt so much pride in the way he had raised his friend up from barbarism. "How quickly have I fallen!" thought Tarzan; but in his heart he did not consider it a fall. Rather, he pitied the poor Parisians, penned up like prisoners in their silly clothes, and watched by policemen all their poor lives, to make sure they did not do anything interesting or exciting.

A two-hour march brought them close to where the elephants had been seen the previous day. From there on they moved very quietly until they found the unmistakable trail along which the herd had passed just hours before. Switching to single file, they followed it for about half an hour. It was Tarzan who first raised his hand to signal that the quarry was near—he had scented the elephants. The others were skeptical when he told them how he knew.

"Come with me," said Tarzan quietly, "and we shall see."

Like a squirrel he sprang into a tree and climbed quickly to the top. One of the nimblest young warriors followed more slowly and carefully. When he had reached a lofty limb beside the ape-man, the latter pointed southward. Sure enough, a few hundred yards away, there were a number of huge gray backs swaying back and forth above the tall jungle grasses. He pointed the direction to the watchers below, indicating with his fingers the number of beasts he could count. Immediately the hunters started toward the elephants. The youthful warrior in the tree hastened down, but Tarzan traveled through the middle terrace of the jungle trees in his ape-like manner.

To hunt wild elephants with primitive weapons requires tremendous hunting skill. Tarzan knew that few native tribes had this ability, and he was proud to associate with one of those few. Already he was beginning to think of himself as a member of the community.

Moving silently overhead, he saw the warriors below silently encircling the unsuspecting herd. When they were within sight of the elephants, they singled out two large tuskers, and at a signal the fifty men rose from their concealment and hurled heavy war spears at the two marked beasts. Their aim was perfect—no one missed. Each animal now carried twenty-five spears in its side.

One never moved, for two perfectly aimed spears had found its heart, and it collapsed without a struggle. The other, standing nearly head-on toward the hunters, was wounded—but not mortally. For a moment the huge bull stood trumpeting in rage and pain, looking wildly about for its tormentor. In accordance with their standard method, the Africans had faded back into the jungle before the great bull's weak eyes could spot them.

However, he caught the sound of their retreat, and with a terrific crashing of underbrush, Tantor, the elephant, charged toward the noise.

Tantor happened to head in the direction of Busuli, and quickly gained on him. Tarzan had been watching from a nearby tree. Seeing his friend's peril, he raced toward the infuriated bull with loud cries, hoping to distract him. It was a waste of precious time, for Tantor's pain and rage made him deaf and blind to anything but the object of his fury. Only a miracle could save Busuli.

With the same disdain for death as when he had hunted Numa, Tarzan hurled himself into the path of Tantor, the elephant, his spear at the ready. All the beast saw was a lighter-brown warrior drop into his path. With a vicious lunge Tantor swerved to dispose of this brazen new enemy who dared to stand between him and his victim. Tantor, however, had not reckoned on Tarzan's lightning quickness, capable of baffling far keener eyes than an elephant's. Before Tantor realized what was happening, Tarzan had driven his finely-crafted iron spearpoint into the massive shoulder and to the heart. The huge tusker toppled to his death at the feet of the ape-man.

Busuli had been too busy running to witness his own rescue, but Waziri and several of the other warriors had seen it all. They hailed Tarzan with delight as they swarmed around him and his immense kill. When he leaped upon the mighty carcass, and gave full voice to his cry of victory, they shrank back in confusion and awe. They knew this as the cry of brutal Bolgani, whom they feared as much as they feared Numa, the lion. Its manlike owner had weird, amazing powers they had never before seen.

But when Tarzan lowered his head and smiled down on them they were reassured, though they did not understand. Nor did they ever fully understand this strange creature who ran through the trees like Manu, the monkey, yet was even more at home on the ground than themselves. They saw that Tarzan was like them except for color, yet as powerful as ten of them, and a match for the fiercest creatures of the jungle.

When the rest of the warriors had gathered, the elephant hunt was resumed. They had covered a bare hundred yards when, from behind them at a great distance, they heard a strange and faint popping.

For an instant they froze to listen intently. Then Tarzan spoke. "Guns!" he said. "The village is being attacked."

"Come!" cried Waziri. "The Arab raiders must have returned to steal our ivory and our women!"

CHAPTER 16

The Ivory Raiders

Spurred by the sharp cracking of gunfire, Waziri's warriors hurried the five miles home to defend their village. When the noise gradually died down, it could only mean one thing: the village's weak defenses had already been overwhelmed.

The returning hunters had gone a little more than three miles when they met the first refugees: a dozen women and youths. They were almost too excited to coherently tell Waziri of the calamity that had befallen his people.

"They are as many as the leaves of the forest," cried one of the women. "There are many Arabs and many more Manyuema, all with guns. They rushed in on us with many shouts, shooting down men, women and children. Most were killed, but those who could fled into the jungle. I do not know if they took any prisoners; they did not seem to want any. The Manyuema called us many names, and said they would kill us all in revenge. I ran away too quickly to hear much more.

The march now resumed with greater stealth,

for Waziri knew that it was too late for anything but revenge. Over the next mile, they picked up a hundred more fugitives, including many warriors to augment their fighting strength. As they neared home, a dozen warriors were sent to scout ahead. Waziri remained with the main body, with Tarzan at his side, as they advanced through the forest.

Presently one of the scouts returned. "The raiders are all within the palisade," he whispered.

"Good!" said Waziri. "We shall charge and slay them all," and he prepared to lead the charge.

"Wait!" cautioned Tarzan. "If they have even fifty guns we shall be slaughtered. Let me go alone to scout from the trees. We may accomplish more by cunning than by force. Will you wait, Waziri?"

"Yes," said the old chief. "Go!"

So Tarzan sprang into the trees and disappeared in the direction of the village. He moved cautiously, to avoid the deadly guns. And when Tarzan of the Apes chose stealth, he had no equal in all the jungle.

In five minutes he had worked his way to the great tree that overhung the palisade at one end of the village. He counted fifty Arabs and perhaps five times as many Manyuema, looting the village and chaining up captives. Tarzan realized that to charge into the face of guns firing from inside the palisade would be futile. He returned to Waziri and advised him to wait, and explained that he, Tarzan, had a better plan.

A moment before, however, a refugee had told Waziri of the atrocious murder of the old chief's wife. Crazed with rage, the elderly warrior-chief cast caution to the winds. Ignoring Tarzan, he summoned his warriors, and commanded them to charge. Yelling savagely and brandishing spears, the little force of barely a hundred warriors rushed toward the village gate.

Before they were halfway there, the Arabs opened up a withering fire from the safety of the palisade. Waziri fell with the first volley, and the charge slackened. Men kept falling; a few reached the gates and were immediately slain. Soon the attack dissolved and the remaining warriors scampered back into the forest with the raiders in hot pursuit. Tarzan had been among the last to retreat, turning now and then to send an arrow into the body of a pursuer.

Once within the jungle, he found a little knot of determined warriors waiting to fight the oncoming horde, but Tarzan had another idea. "I will lead you to victory. But first, scatter through the forest, picking up as many stragglers as you can find. At night, work your way to the spot where we killed the elephants today. Then I will explain my plan. You are too few to defeat the Arabs and the Manyuema through normal means."

They finally assented. "When you scatter," explained Tarzan in conclusion, "your foes will have to scatter to follow you. As they do, make them pay: shoot them from behind trees."

The tribe had barely time to get moving before the first of the raiders had crossed the clearing in pursuit of them. Tarzan ran a short distance and then took to the trees. He climbed to the upper terrace and doubled back toward the village. Here he found that almost every Arab and Manyuema had joined in the pursuit, leaving the village deserted except for the chained prisoners and a single gate-guard.

The sentry stood watching the jungle, and did not see Tarzan drop to the ground at the far end of the village street. With drawn bow the ape-man stalked his unsuspecting victim. The prisoners had already seen him, and their eyes filled with wonder and with hope. He halted ten paces behind the guard, drew the arrow back, and with a sudden *twang* he sent it home. The sentry sank silently forward onto his face, an arrow all the way through his heart.

Then Tarzan turned his attention to the fifty women and youths chained neck to neck. There was no way to release the ancient padlocks in such a short time, so the ape-man called to them to follow him as they were. He took the gun and cartridge-belt from the dead sentry and led the grateful band out the gate and into the jungle.

It was a slow and difficult march, with much stumbling and falling due to the uncomfortable chains. Tarzan also had made a wide detour to stay well clear of any returning raiders. He heard occasional shots, so the Arab slavers were obviously chasing the warriors. He hoped they were ambushing the marauders when possible.

Toward dusk the firing ceased entirely, and Tarzan surmised that the raiders had all returned to the village. He smiled, knowing how enraged they would be to find their sentry dead and their prisoners rescued! It would have made them angrier had he been able to bring along some of the village's ivory, but it would have been a terrible burden for the rescued women. In any event, he planned to make sure the Arabs did not get to keep any ivory.

It was after midnight when Tarzan brought his slow-moving caravan to the spot where the elephants lay, guided by the sight of fire. The villagers had been hard at work clearing the area and constructing an African *boma*—a thorny ring of brush—within which they had built a huge bonfire for warmth and safety.

As they neared the encampment, Tarzan hailed the *boma* to let them know that friends were coming. The reception was joyous; they had all been thought lost forever, along with Tarzan. While many wanted to stay up all night feasting on the elephant meat, others knew better: they must get what sleep they could. Tomorrow would be a long, hard day for everyone. Even so, sleep would be difficult, for many women wept for family members lost in the massacre. Finally Tarzan managed to calm the sound, if not the sorrow, by pointing out that loud crying would surely attract the Arabs.

When dawn came Tarzan explained his battle plan, and all agreed that it was the safest and surest way to wipe out the marauders and avenge their dead. First the women and children, guarded by some twenty aging and very young warriors, were sent southward out of danger. They were to set up a *boma*, for they might have to remain there for days or even weeks. The main force of warriors then left for the village.

By two hours after daylight, a thin circle of warriors watched the occupied palisade. Here and there one was perched high in a tree. Presently a Manyuema within the village fell, pierced by a single arrow. There had been no war-cries, no waving of spears—just a silent messenger of death from the forest.

The Arabs and their followers were thrown into a fine rage. They ran for the gates, to brutally punish this outrage, but had no idea where their foes were. As they stood bickering angrily, one of the Arabs sank silently to the ground in their very midst with a thin arrow protruding from his heart.

Tarzan had placed the finest marksmen in the surrounding trees, with directions only to fire when the enemy was facing away. After an archer shot, he would slink behind the trunk of his tree, to wait until no one was looking toward him. Three times the Arabs started across the clearing in what they believed was the right direction, but each time an arrow got another of them from behind. Finally they launched a determined search of the forest. Their enemies melted away, leaving the Arabs no sign.

But above them still lurked Tarzan of the Apes.

Presently a Manyuema forged ahead of his companions, but a moment later those behind stumbled over their comrade's dead body, an arrow through his heart. There was no way to tell where the shot had come from.

Guerrilla warfare can wrack the nerves, and indeed the Manyuema soon began to panic. Anyone who got separated from the rest was soon found dead with an arrow in the heart. Worst of all, not once this morning had they actually seen an enemy—just the pitiless arrows.

When they finally returned to the village it was no better. Every now and then another man would pitch forward in death. The Manyuema pressured their Arab masters to flee this terrible place, but the Arabs were unwilling. They did not wish to march laden down with ivory while being picked off one by one, nor were they willing to leave that fortune behind.

Finally the entire expedition sought sanctuary in the thatched huts. Tarzan made note of the hut where the chief Arabs had gone, balanced himself on an overhanging limb and launched a spear with all his might. The missile tore through the thatch of the roof, and a howl of pain told him he had hit someone. Having demonstrated to the marauders that nowhere in the compound was safe, Tarzan returned to the jungle. He collected the other warriors and withdrew a mile to the south to rest and eat, posting sentries in the trees above. No pursuit came—and small wonder.

An inspection of his force showed not a single wound. The Africans estimated that no fewer than twenty of the enemy had been slain. They were elated, and some of the younger men wanted to finish the day with a glorious rush upon the village. They would slaughter their enemies, with special treatment reserved for the hated Manyuema. The older warriors disagreed, wishing to continue the current tactics.

Eventually Tarzan joined the debate by addressing the hotheads: "It would be crazy to launch a frontal assault. Has our new method not proven successful? You are master archers. Have you not already killed twenty of the enemy without a single scratch to you? I understand Waziri's fury, and why he charged, but we lost a dozen men that way without taking down a single Arab or Manyuema. If we do that again, we will all die, and what will become of our people? And furthermore, if you assault in this way, I will not remain, but will return to my own country."

This swayed the fighting blood of even the young warriors, for Tarzan's leadership had gained results. They agreed to continue the guerrilla tactics if he would promise to remain.

"Very well," he said. "Let us return to the elephant *boma* for the night. I plan to give the Arabs a little taste of what awaits them if they remain in our country. If they suffer no more today, they will feel reassured. Then, when we frighten them again, the terror will be doubled."

So they marched back to the elephant-hunt camp, lit a great fire, ate, and told of the day's adventures. Tarzan slept until midnight, then arose and crept into the ebony darkness of the forest.

An hour later he came to the edge of the village clearing. There was a campfire burning within the palisade. The ape-man crept across the clearing to stand before the barred gates, through which he saw a lone sentry sitting by the fire.

Quietly, Tarzan went to the tree at the end of the village street. He climbed softly to his place, and readied an arrow. For several minutes he tried to draw a good bead on the sentry, but the light and the flickering branches were a problem—his plan depended upon the sentry's sudden, silent death.

In addition to his bow, arrows and rope, the ape-man had also brought the gun captured the day before. Stashing all of these in a convenient tree-fork, he dropped lightly to the ground with only his long knife. The dozing sentry's back was toward him. Like a cat, Tarzan crept up on the man. He was within two paces of him now—another instant and the knife would slide silently into the fellow's heart.

Tarzan crouched, ready to spring—the quickest and surest attack of the jungle beast—when the sentry, warned by some subtle sense, sprang to his feet and faced the ape-man.

CHAPTER 17

The White Chief of the Waziri

When the Manyuema sentry saw the strange, knife-wielding ghost, his only thought was to escape the giant who had arrived out of nowhere. Before he could turn, Tarzan was upon him. A great hand crushed the sentry's windpipe before he could think to scream for aid, forcing him earthward. The Manyuema battled furiously for his life, even bravely, but the awful fingers choked the life from him. His tongue shot out, and soon he convulsed and lay still in death.

The ape-man threw the body across a broad shoulder, collected his gun, and trotted silently up the sleeping village street toward the tree that he found so useful. He carried the dead sentry up into the foliage.

First he stripped the body of cartridge belt and ornaments, wedging the corpse into a convenient tree-fork. Then he took the man's gun and walked far out onto a limb where he could see the huts better. Taking careful aim at the chief Arabs' hut, he pulled the trigger. The answering groan brought a smile to Tarzan's lips—another lucky hit!

After a moment's silence in camp, Manyuema and Arabs alike came pouring from the huts like a swarm of angry hornets. In reality they were more frightened than angry; the single shot in the night shattered the strained nerves of both African and Arab alike, and now they believed themselves doomed. Finding the sentry absent, and with no other idea what to do, they began to blast away at the barred village gates. Tarzan took advantage of the noise and confusion to fire into the mob below.

No one heard his shot above the general racket, but some Manyuema saw one of their number crumple suddenly to the earth in their midst, dead. They panicked, and it took all the brutal authority of the Arabs to keep them from rushing helter-skelter into the jungle—anywhere to escape from this terrible village.

After a time they began to quiet down, and to take heart again, but not for long. Just as they began to relax, Tarzan let forth a weird moan. As the raiders looked up to find the sound, the ape-man threw the sentry's body far out above their heads.

With howls of alarm the throng broke in all directions to escape this new and terrible creature. The body of the sentry, falling with wide-sprawled arms and legs, looked like a great beast of prey. In their haste to escape, many of the Manyuema scaled the palisade, while others tore open the gates and rushed madly out toward the jungle. Those Arabs and Manyuema who remained within the palisade dove for cover.

For a time no one investigated the falling object, but Tarzan knew that they soon would. When they discovered that it was only the dead sentry, he was pretty sure what they would do next. He faded silently away back toward the camp of the Waziri warriors.

Presently, one of the Arabs turned and saw that whatever had leaped from the tree lay still and quiet where it had fallen. Cautiously he crept back toward it, and saw that it was but a man. A moment later he was beside the figure, recognizing it as the corpse of the Manyuema sentry.

His companions came rapidly at his call, and after a moment's excited conversation they did precisely what Tarzan had expected. Raising their guns to their shoulders, they poured volley after volley into the tree from which the corpse had come. If Tarzan had remained there he would have been riddled by a hundred bullets.

Further examination of the dead sentry frightened them even more, for the only marks of violence on the corpse were giant fingerprints on the swollen throat. It was bad enough that they were not even safe behind the palisade, but for an enemy to enter it unseen and kill their sentry with bare hands was beyond all reason. The Manyuema blamed their ill luck on evil spirits. The Arabs had no better explanation to offer.

With at least fifty of their number fleeing through the jungle night, and with no idea when the sniping might resume, it was a desperate band of cutthroats that waited sleeplessly for the dawn. Only a promise from the Arabs that they would all depart at dawn kept the rest of the Manyuema from joining their fleeing fellows in the night, for they were beginning to fear the unknown killers even more greatly than they did their cruel masters.

And so, when Tarzan and his warriors returned to the attack the next morning, they found the raiders about to march out of the village, the Manyuema laden with stolen ivory. Tarzan grinned from his high perch in the tall trees; they would not carry it far.

Then he saw something worrisome: a number of the Manyuema were lighting torches in the remnant of the campfire. They were about to burn the village.

Tarzan cupped his hands, and called loudly in Arabic: "Do not set fire to the huts, or we shall kill you all! Do not set fire to the huts, or we shall kill you all!" He repeated this a dozen times.

The Manyuema hesitated, then one of them flung his torch back into the campfire. The others were about to follow suit when an Arab began to beat them toward the huts with a stick, ordering them to proceed with the arson. Tarzan stood up on the swaying branch a hundred feet above the ground, raised a gun to his shoulder, took careful aim and fired. The Arab with the stick fell dead in his tracks, and another batch of Manyuema threw away their torches and fled from the village. Their former masters knelt on the ground and fired at them as they raced toward the jungle.

But however angry the Arabs might have been at their slaves' rebellion, they were at least convinced that it would be a bad idea to set fire to the village after all. In their hearts, they swore to return again with enough force to sweep this whole country clear of all human life.

They had looked in vain for the Arabic-speaking voice, but could not locate its source. They had seen the puff of smoke from the tree following the sniper's shot, and had immediately fired a volley into it, but with no indication of having hit anything. Tarzan had known better than to stay around. The *crack* of his rifle shot had scarcely echoed away before he was on the ground and racing for another tree a hundred yards away, from which he could watch the raiders' activities. It then occurred to him that there was more fun to be had with the raiders, so he cupped his hands again.

"Leave the ivory!" he cried in the East African language used by the Waziri and Manyuema. "Leave the ivory! Dead men have no use for ivory!"

Some of the Manyuema started to lay down their loads, but this was too much for the Arabs.

With loud shouts and curses they trained their guns upon the bearers, threatening instant death to any who set down his load. To abandon this enormous fortune seemed a fate worse than death to the Arab slavers.

And so they marched out of the village of the Waziri, their slaves bearing the ivory ransom of two dozen kings. They headed north, back toward their settlement beyond the Congo deep in the African jungle.

On either side of them traveled an invisible and relentless foe.

One runner was sent to the temporary *boma* to tell the women and children that they could return home. Then, under Tarzan's guidance, the Waziri warriors stationed themselves along the trail in the densest underbrush at far intervals. As the column passed, a well-aimed single arrow or heavy spear would pierce a Manyuema or an Arab. Then the Waziri marksman would melt into the distance and run ahead to set up a new ambush farther on. They struck only where success was sure and detection all but impossible, and their aim was superb.

The slow-moving column was constantly near panic—they could not know who would fall next, or when. A dozen times the Manyuema were ready to drop their burdens and flee north, and it took all of the Arabs' effort to prevent this. The day wore on: a nightmare for the raiders, a weary but successful one for the Waziri. At night the Arabs had their slaves built a crude *boma* in a clearing by a river, and there they encamped.

At intervals during the night a rifle would bark close above their heads, and one of the dozen sentries they had posted would collapse. At this rate it was clear that they would be wiped out one by one. Even so, the persistent greed of the Arabs made them cling to their loot. That morning, they again forced the demoralized Manyuema to hoist their deadly burdens and stagger on into the jungle.

For three days the plodding column suffered onward. Each hour was marked by its deadly arrow or cruel spear. The nights were made sleepless and terrifying by the barking of the invisible gun that made sentry duty a death sentence.

On the morning of the fourth day, the Manyuema refused to lift the ivory until the Arabs shot two of them. As they did, a voice rang out, clear and strong, in the East African dialect: "Today you die, oh Manyuema, unless you lay down the ivory. You have guns; why do you not use them? Kill the Arabs, end your slavery, and we will not harm you. We will take you back to our village and feed you, and lead you out of our country in safety and in peace. Fall upon your masters, and we will help you. Remain slaves, and you will die!"

As the voice died down the raiders stood frozen. The Arabs and their Manyuema slaves eyed one another, waiting for someone to act first.

There were some thirty Arabs left, and about one hundred and fifty Africans, all armed—even those carrying tusks had rifles slung across their backs.

The Arabs drew together. Their leader raised his rifle and ordered the Manyuema to take up the march. But at the same instant one of the Africans threw down his load, took his rifle in hand, and fired point-blank at the Arabs. In an instant the camp was a cursing, howling brawl with guns and knives and pistols. The Arabs fought determinedly but hopelessly. The rain of lead pouring into them from their rebelling slaves combined with the shower of arrows and spears from the jungle— aimed solely at the Arabs—could have only one outcome. In ten minutes the last Arab lay dead.

When the firing had ceased Tarzan spoke again to the Manyuema:

"Take up the ivory you stole from our village, and return it. We shall not harm you."

For a moment the Manyuema hesitated. They had no desire to walk that trail again.
They talked together in low whispers, and one called aloud into the jungle:

"How do we know that you will not kill us all afterward?" he asked.

"You have only our promise," replied Tarzan. "But you do know that we can kill you all on this trail if we wish. We are only likely to do that if you anger us."

"Who are you that speaks the tongue of

Arabs?" cried the Manyuema spokesman. "Let us see you, and then we shall answer you."

Tarzan stepped out of the jungle a dozen paces from them. "Then look!" he said. They were shocked to see that he was white, for never had they seen a white man in full African dress, much less one so powerfully built.

"You may trust me," said Tarzan. "If you do as I say, and harm none of my people, we shall not harm you. Will you return our ivory to our village in peace, or shall we continue to follow you along your trail toward the north?"

The Manyuema had no desire for more days like the past three. After a short conference, they took up their burdens and began to retrace their steps toward the village of the Waziri. At the end of the third day they marched into the village gate with their valuable cargoes.

The Manyuema were greeted by the survivors of the recent massacre. It took all of Tarzan's persuasion and influence to keep the Waziri from tearing the Manyuema to pieces. When he explained that he had given his word, and reminded them of their complete victory, they finally allowed the hated Manyuema to rest unharmed inside their palisade.

That night the village warriors met to celebrate their victories, and to choose a new chief. Until now there had been no time to choose a new chief in council, but it could wait no longer. The senior warriors sat in a circle around a small fire to discuss the matter. They agreed that the strange white man's leadership had enabled them to regain their village and prevent much loss of life, in contrast to the suicidal charge Waziri had led. The older warriors, wiser in strategy, saw the long-term value of clever tactics over brave, blind charges. Then Busuli spoke:

"Since Waziri is dead, leaving no son, only one among us is fit to make us a good king. Only one man's tactics bring us easy victory against the guns of the Arabs, and without the loss of a single life, and that is the white man who has led us for the past few days," and Busuli sprang to his feet. With uplifted spear, in a crouch, he began to dance slowly about Tarzan, chanting in time to his steps: "Waziri, king of the Waziri; Waziri, killer of Arabs; Waziri, king of the Waziri."

One by one the other warriors joined Busuli in the dance, signifying their acceptance of Tarzan. The women came and began to drum around the rim of the circle, joining in the chant. In the center of the circle sat Tarzan of the Apes—now Waziri, king of the Waziri. For, like his predecessor, he was to take the name of his tribe as his own.

The dance grew faster, louder and more frenzied. Spears were brandished; shields were beaten against the hard-packed earth of the village street. As the excitement built, the ape-man sprang to his feet and joined in the wild ceremony. In the center of the circle he leaped and roared and shook his heavy spear with the same abandon as the rest. The last remnant of his civilization was forgotten—he was a primitive man to the fullest now; reveling in the freedom of the fierce, wild life he loved, a king in Africa.

Would Olga de Coude have recognized the well-dressed, quiet young man with his well-bred face and refined manners? And Jane Porter! Would she have still loved this savage warrior chieftain, dancing naked among his equally naked subjects? And D'Arnot! Was this the man D'Arnot had introduced into half a dozen of the most exclusive clubs of Paris? What would the House of Lords have said if a member pointed to this dancing giant, in his tribal regalia, and said: "There, my lords, is John Clayton, the Lord Greystoke."

And so Tarzan of the Apes was again a king—this time, among men.

CHAPTER 18

The Lottery of Death

Jane Porter was the first in the lifeboat to wake up the morning after the wreck of the *Lady Alice*. To her alarm, she realized that they had become separated from the other boats. Gazing at the vast expanse of empty ocean gave her a great sense of utter loneliness and doom.

After a while Clayton woke up, too. It was several minutes before he fully realized his situation. Finally his bewildered eyes fell upon his fiancée.

"Jane!" he cried. "Thank God that we are together!"

"Look," she said, pointing to the horizon. "We are all alone."

Clayton scanned the water in every direction.

"Where can they be?" he cried. "They cannot have gone down, for the sea has been calm, and they were afloat after the yacht sank—I saw them all."

He awoke the other members of the party, and explained their plight.

"Just as well the boats are scattered, sir," said

one of the sailors. "Means a much better chance that one will be found, and then they'll search for the others."

They were briefly cheered by the good sense of this, but only momentarily, for it was soon discovered that the sailors who had last been at the oars had fallen asleep and lost their oars into the sea; now they were nowhere to be found. The sailors nearly fought over the matter, but Clayton succeeded in quieting them. A moment later Monsieur Thuran almost started another fight with a nasty remark about the stupidity of all Englishmen, and especially English sailors.

"Come, come, mates," spoke up one of the men, Tompkins, who had taken no part in the fight, "squabblin' won't get us nothin'. As Spider 'ere said before, we'll all bloody well be picked up. Let's eat, sez I."

"That's not a bad idea," said Monsieur Thuran, and then, turning to the third sailor, Wilson, he said, "Pass one of those tins aft, my good man."

"Fetch it yerself," retorted Wilson sullenly. "I ain't a-takin' no orders from no Frenchie—you ain't captain o' this ship."

Eventually Clayton himself had to get the tin, and then another angry exchange ensued when one of the sailors accused Clayton and Monsieur Thuran of conspiring to control the provisions so that they could eat the most.

"Someone should take command of this boat," spoke up Jane Porter, thoroughly disgusted. "It is terrible enough to be alone in a frail boat on the Atlantic, without the added misery and danger of constant bickering and brawling among ourselves. You men should elect a leader, and then do as he says."

Her words temporarily quieted the men, and finally they decided to divide the two kegs of water and the four tins of food into two parts, half going forward to the three sailors to use as they chose, and the balance to the three passengers. When the provisions had been passed out, each group started to break out food and water. The sailors were the first to get one of the tins open, and they cursed in rage and disappointment.

"What is the trouble now?" asked Clayton.

"Trouble!" shrieked Spider. "Trouble! It's worse than trouble—it's death! This bloomin' tin is full of coal oil!"

Hastily now Clayton and Monsieur Thuran tore open one of theirs, only to learn the grim truth that it also contained coal oil. The rest of the tins were quickly opened, all to howls of anger. There was not an ounce of food aboard.

"Well, thank Gawd it wasn't the water," cried Thompkins. "It's easier to get along without food than water. We can eat our shoes if worse comes to worst, but we couldn't drink 'em."

As he spoke Wilson had been boring a hole in

one of the water kegs, and Spider held a tin cup to catch the precious fluid. A thin stream of dry black particles filtered slowly out into the bottom of the cup. With a groan Wilson dropped the keg, and sat staring horrified at the dry substance.

"The kegs are filled with gunpowder," said Spider, in a low tone, turning to those aft. And so they all proved to be.

"Coal oil and gunpowder!" cried Monsieur Thuran. "Saints! What a diet for shipwrecked mariners!"

Knowing now that there was neither food nor water on board, the pangs of hunger and thirst worsened immediately. The full horrors of shipwreck were upon them.

Days passed in misery. Aching eyes scanned the horizon day and night until the weakening watchers would sink exhausted to the bottom of the boat. Only in sleep was there relief from the miserable reality. The starving sailors ate their leather belts, their shoes, even the sweatbands from their caps, although both Clayton and Monsieur Thuran had tried to convince them that these would only make them sick.

Weak and hopeless, the entire party lay beneath the pitiless tropical sun, with parched lips and swollen tongues, waiting for the death they were beginning to crave. The intense suffering of the first few days had become deadened for the three passengers who had eaten nothing, but the agony of the sailors was worse, as their weak stomachs attempted to digest the bits of leather they had eaten.

Tompkins was the first to succumb. Just a week after the *Lady Alice* went down, the sailor went into frightful convulsions and then died. For hours his pain-contorted features lay grinning back at the others, until Jane Porter could endure it no longer. "Can you not drop his body overboard, William?" she asked.

Clayton rose and staggered toward the corpse. The two remaining sailors eyed him with a strange, baleful light in their sunken eyes. Futilely the Englishman tried to lift the corpse over the side of the boat, but he was too weak. "Lend me a hand here, please," he said to Wilson, who lay nearest him.

"Wot do you want to throw 'im over for?" questioned the sailor.

"We've got to do it before we're too weak," replied Clayton. "He'd be awful by tomorrow, after a day under that broiling sun."

"Better leave well enough alone," grumbled Wilson. "We may need him before tomorrow."

Slowly Clayton began to realize the fellow's reason for objecting. "God!" whispered Clayton, in a horrified tone. "You cannot mean—"

"W'y not?" growled Wilson. "Ain't we gotta live? He's dead. He won't care."

"Come here, Thuran," said Clayton, turning toward the Russian. "We'll have something worse than death aboard if we don't get rid of this body before dark."

Wilson staggered up menacingly to prevent the act, but when his comrade, Spider, sided with Clayton and Monsieur Thuran he gave up, and sat eying the corpse hungrily as the three men's combined efforts succeeded in rolling it overboard.

The rest of the day Wilson sat glaring at Clayton, eyes gleaming with insanity. Toward evening he started chuckling and mumbling to himself, but his eyes never left Clayton. After it became quite dark Clayton could still feel those terrible eyes upon him, and tried to remain awake. Eventually he lost the battle and fell asleep.

By the time a shuffling noise reawakened Clayton, the moon had risen. As he opened his startled eyes he saw Wilson creeping toward him, his mouth open and his swollen tongue hanging out.

The slight noise had also awakened Jane Porter, and she gave a shrill cry of alarm. At the same instant the sailor lurched forward and fell upon Clayton. Like a wild beast his teeth sought Clayton's throat, but his intended victim somehow found sufficient strength to hold the maniac's mouth away.

Jane Porter's scream woke up Monsieur Thuran and Spider. On seeing the cause of her alarm, both men crawled to Clayton's rescue, and the three of them were able to subdue Wilson. For a few minutes he lay chattering and laughing in the bottom of the boat, and then with an awful scream he staggered to his feet. Before anyone could stop him, he had leaped overboard.

The incident was too much for them. Spider broke down and wept; Jane Porter prayed; Clayton swore softly to himself; and Monsieur Thuran sat with his head in his hands, thinking.

The next morning, he had a proposal for Spider and Clayton.

"Gentlemen," said Monsieur Thuran, "you see what awaits us all unless we are picked up within a day or two. There is little hope. We have not seen any sail, nor even the faintest smudge of smoke. Without food there is no chance; with food there might be. We must choose swiftly: either we all die together within a few days, or one must be sacrificed that the others may live. Do you quite clearly grasp my meaning?"

Jane Porter was horrified. She would have expected such an idea from a poor, ignorant sailor, perhaps, but not from someone who posed as a gentleman of culture and refinement.

"Better that we die together, then," said Clayton.

"That is for the majority to decide," replied Monsieur Thuran. "As only one of us three will be the object of sacrifice, we shall decide. Miss Porter is in no danger."

"How shall we know who is to be first?" asked Spider.

"We can draw lots," replied Monsieur Thuran. "I have a number of franc pieces in my pocket. We can choose one with a certain date—whoever draws this date shall be the first."

"I shall have nothing to do with any such wicked plan," muttered Clayton. "We might yet sight land or a ship in time."

"You will do as the majority decide, or you will be 'the first' without the formality of drawing lots," said Monsieur Thuran threateningly. "Come, let us vote on the plan; I am in favor of it. How about you, Spider?"

"And I," replied the sailor.

"The majority wins," announced Monsieur Thuran, "and now let us draw lots. So that three may live, one of us must die perhaps a few hours sooner than otherwise."

Then he began preparing for the lottery of death, while Jane Porter sat in wide-eyed horror. Monsieur Thuran spread his coat out on the bottom of the boat, and then from a handful of money he selected six one-franc pieces. The other two men bent close above him as he inspected them. Finally he handed them all to Clayton.

"Look at them carefully," he said. "The oldest date is eighteen-seventy-five, and there is only one of that year."

Clayton and the sailor could detect no difference other than the dates, and were quite satisfied. They would have been far less pleased had they known of Monsieur Thuran's past experience as a gambler. His sense of touch was so fine that he could almost tell cards apart by their mere feel. The 1875 coin was a hair thinner than the rest, but neither Clayton nor Spider could have detected it by touch or sight.

"In what order shall we draw?" asked Monsieur Thuran. From past experience, he knew that men tended to prefer to draw last in such situations, so he offered to draw first. His hand was under the coat for only as long as it took his deft fingers to find and discard the fatal piece. He brought forth an 1888 coin.

Then Clayton drew. Jane Porter leaned forward tensely as her fiancé's hand groped about beneath the coat. Presently he withdrew it, a one-franc coin lying in his palm. For an instant he dared not look, but Monsieur Thuran, who had leaned nearer to see the date, exclaimed that he was safe.

Jane Porter sank weak and trembling against the side of the boat. She felt sick, and if Spider did not now draw the 1875 piece, she must endure the whole horrid thing again.

The sailor already had his hand beneath the coat. Sweat beaded upon his brow, and he trembled. He cursed himself aloud for having taken the last draw, for now his chances for escape were but three to one, whereas Monsieur Thuran's had been five to one, and Clayton's four to one.

The Russian was very patient, and did not hurry the man, for he knew that he himself was quite safe. When the sailor withdrew his hand and looked at the piece of money within, he fainted to the bottom of the boat. Both Clayton and Monsieur Thuran hastened weakly to examine the coin, which had rolled loose.

It was dated 1902.

Now the whole wretched process must be repeated. Once more the Russian drew forth a harmless coin. Jane Porter closed her eyes as Clayton reached beneath the coat. Spider bent, wide-eyed, toward the hand that was to decide his fate. Then William Cecil Clayton, Lord Greystoke, removed his hand from beneath the coat, and with a coin tight pressed within his palm where none might see it, he looked at Jane Porter. He did not dare open his hand.

"Quick!" hissed Spider. "My Gawd, let's see it."

Clayton opened his fingers. Spider was the first to see the date, and before anyone else knew anything, he got to his feet and dove overboard to disappear forever into the green depths of the ocean. The coin bore the date 1899. They had gotten the death without its horrid benefit.

The strain had exhausted the three remaining castaways so greatly that they lay half passed out for the rest of the day. Several more days of increasing weakness and hopelessness passed. At length Monsieur Thuran crawled to where

Clayton lay.

"We must draw once more before we are too weak even to eat," he whispered.

Clayton was by now scarcely able to move. Jane Porter had not spoken for three days.

He knew that she was dying. Horrible as the thought was, he hoped that the sacrifice of either Thuran or himself might give her renewed strength, and so he immediately agreed to the Russian's proposal.

They drew under the same plan as before, but there could be but one result—Clayton drew the 1875 piece.

"When shall it be?" he asked Thuran.

The Russian had already drawn a pocketknife from his trousers, and was weakly attempting to open it. "Now," he muttered, and his greedy eyes gloated upon the Englishman.

"Can't you wait until dark?" asked Clayton. "Miss Porter must not see this done. We were to have been married, you know."

A look of disappointment came over Monsieur Thuran's face.

"Very well," he replied hesitantly. "It will not be long until night. I have waited for many days— I can wait a few hours longer."

"Thank you, my friend," murmured Clayton. "Now I shall go to her side and remain with her until it is time. I would like to have an hour or two with her before I die."

When Clayton reached the girl's side she was comatose, dying. At least she would not have to watch the awful tragedy. He raised her hand to his cracked and swollen lips, then for a long time he lay caressing the thin, clawlike member that had once been the beautiful, shapely hand of a young Baltimore belle.

It was quite dark before he knew it. Soon a voice spoke in the night: the Russian, calling him to his doom.

"I am coming, Monsieur Thuran," he hastened to reply.

Three times he attempted to crawl back to his death, but he had become too weak to return to Thuran's side.

"You will have to come to me, Monsieur," he called weakly. "I have not enough strength to crawl."

"Saints!" muttered Monsieur Thuran. "You are attempting to cheat me out of my winnings!"

Clayton heard the man shuffling about in the bottom of the boat. Finally there was a despairing groan. "I cannot crawl," he heard the Russian wail. "It is too late. You have tricked me, you dirty English dog."

"I have not tricked you, Monsieur," replied Clayton. "I have done my best to rise, but I shall try again, and if you will try possibly each of us can crawl halfway. Then you shall have your 'winnings.'"

Again Clayton strained his utmost, and he

heard Thuran apparently doing the same. Nearly an hour later the Englishman succeeded in raising himself to his hands and knees, but immediately pitched forward on his face.

A moment later he heard an exclamation of relief from Monsieur Thuran. "I am coming," whispered the Russian.

Again Clayton tried to stagger toward his fate, but once more he fell face-first into the boat's bottom. Try as he might, he could not rise again. He wound up on his back, looking up at the stars, listening to the labored shuffling and pained breathing of the approaching Russian.

It felt like he must have stayed an hour in this way, waiting for the other man to crawl out of the dark and end his misery. Thuran was quite close now, but there were increasingly long pauses between his attempts at movement. He did not seem to be getting much closer.

Finally he knew that Thuran was quite close beside him. Clayton heard a cackling laugh, something touched his face, and he lost consciousness.

CHAPTER 19

The City of Gold

T he very night that Tarzan of the Apes became chief of the Waziri, the woman he loved lay thin and comatose in a tiny boat two hundred miles west of him out on the Atlantic.

The week following Tarzan's rise to the kingship was spent escorting the Manyuema out of Waziri lands, as promised. Before he left them he made them pledge never again to march against the Waziri. They were happy to promise; they had no desire to ever face the new Waziri fighting tactics again.

Almost immediately upon his return to the village, Tarzan began readying an expedition in search of the ruined city of gold described by the old chief. He selected fifty of the sturdiest warriors of his tribe, choosing only the most adventuresome men. The lure of gold was as strong for him as the lure of adventure, for he had learned among civilized men that the possessor of the magic yellow metal could work miracles. He had not yet, however, thought about what he would actually *do* with a fortune in gold in the heart of Africa.

So one glorious tropical morning Waziri, chief of the Waziri, set out at the head of fifty hardy African warriors. They followed the course which the old Waziri had described and for days they marched up one river, across a low divide; down another river; up a third. At the end of the twenty-fifth day they camped on a mountainside, from the summit of which where they hoped to catch their first view of the marvelous city of treasure.

Early the next morning they were climbing the steep crags which formed the last and greatest natural barrier in their path. It was nearly noon before Tarzan, leading the thin line of climbing warriors, scaled the last cliff and stood at the mountaintop.

On either hand towered mighty peaks thousands of feet higher than this one. Behind him stretched the wooded valley through which they had come, across which was the low range marking the boundary of Waziri lands.

Before him lay a shallow, narrow valley dotted with stunted trees and covered with huge boulders. On the far side of the valley lay what appeared to be a mighty city, its great walls, its lofty spires, towers and domes showing red and yellow in the sunlight. Tarzan was too far away to note the signs of ruin; to him it appeared magnificent. He imagined its broad avenues and its huge temples filled with happy, active people.

For an hour the little expedition rested, then Tarzan led them down into the valley. It was still light when they halted before the towering walls of the ancient city.

The outer wall was fifty feet high where it had not partly fallen, but nowhere was it lower than thirty feet. It was still a strong defense. Several times Tarzan had thought he saw something moving behind the ruined portions of the wall nearest them, as though creatures were watching them from inside.

That night they camped outside the city. Once, at midnight, they were awakened by a shrill scream from behind the great wall. It was very high at first, dying down gradually into a series of dismal moans. It badly frightened the tribesmen, and it was an hour before the camp settled back down to sleep. In the morning, some of the Waziri cast fearful, sidelong glances at the forbidding structure looming above them. A number of them wanted to give up the quest and hasten back the way they had come, but finally Busuli threatened to enter the city alone with Tarzan if need be. The rest agreed to accompany them

For fifteen minutes they marched along the face of the wall before they discovered a way in: a narrow opening about twenty inches wide. A worn flight of concrete steps were visible in the gloom, disappearing in a sharp turn a few yards inside.

Into this narrow alley, Tarzan made his way,

turning his giant shoulders sideways to squeeze through. His warriors followed as the path wound and twisted through courts and corridors. Soon Tarzan and his warriors found themselves in a broad avenue, looking across at crumbling, vine-covered, forbidding granite buildings. The massive building directly across from them, topped by an enormous dome, seemed better preserved than the other structures. At either side of its great entrance stood rows of tall pillars, each capped by a huge, strange bird carved from solid rock.

As the adventurers gazed in wonder at this ancient city in the midst of wild Africa, several of them noticed movement within the structure ahead. Shadowy shapes appeared to be moving about in the semi-dark interior. It was eerie—living things seemed out of place in this weird, dead ruin of a city.

Tarzan recalled having read in the Paris library about a lost race of white men that native legend described as living in the heart of Africa. Perhaps these were the ruins of that civilization. Could it be that a remnant of that lost people still inhabit-ed the ruin of this once mighty city? Again he sensed a stealthy movement within the great tem-ple before him. "Come!" he said to his Waziri. "Let us have a look behind those ruined walls."

Some of the men were unwilling, but the example of his confident entrance inspired them all to follow along. Another shriek like the one last

night might be enough to send them racing for the narrow opening and back to the world they knew.

As Tarzan entered the building he sensed many eyes upon him. There was a rustling in the shadows nearby, and he could have sworn that he saw a human hand moving above him up near the domed ceiling. The floor of the chamber was of concrete, the walls of smooth granite, carved with strange figures of men and beasts. Tablets of gold bearing strange symbols were set in the solid masonry of the walls. They passed through several more chambers, finding evidence of fabulous wealth. In one room were seven pillars of solid gold, and in another the floor itself was of the precious metal. While he explored, his bravest warriors huddled close behind him, keeping an uneasy watch.

The strain began to tell upon the nerves of the Waziri, and many of them asked Tarzan to return to the sunlight. "The spirits of the dead are watching us, O king," whispered Busuli. "They are waiting until they have led us deep inside their stronghold, and then they will attack us and tear us to pieces with their teeth. That is the way with spirits. My mother's uncle, who is a great shaman, has told me about it many times." A few brash younger warriors wanted to stay, but most expressed readiness to leave.

Tarzan laughed. "Go back into the sunlight, my people," he said. "I will join you when I have searched this old ruin from top to bottom. Even if I find no more gold, we can take the tablets from the walls, though the pillars are too heavy for us. There should be great storerooms full of gold that we can easily carry away, if I can only find them. Wait for me outside."

Busuli and several others hesitated to leave him, torn between love for their king and fear of the unknown. Finally they accepted the counsel of the older warriors: if their mighty king with the strange abilities wanted to stir up spirits, that was his right, but they had no desire to do so. Nervously, they made their way back outside.

Behind them stood Tarzan of the Apes where they had left him, a grim smile upon his lips, waiting for something to pounce on him. But again silence reigned, except for the faint sound of bare feet moving stealthily nearby.

Then Tarzan continued into the depths of the temple. From room to room he went, until he came to a crude, barred door. As he put his shoulder against it, the terrible shriek of warning from last night rang out almost beside him—and continued. Was he being warned to stay out of this particular room? Or could it hold the secret to the treasure stores?

If it was meant as a warning, it didn't work. Now his desire to explore was tripled. Despite the shrieking, he kept his shoulder to the door until it swung open on creaking wooden hinges.

Inside, all was black as night, with no window to let in the faintest ray of light. Feeling the floor in front of him with the butt of his spear, Tarzan entered the gloom. Suddenly the door closed behind him, and from the darkness hands clutched him from every direction.

The ape-man fought with a savage fury, but there were simply too many, and at last they dragged him down by sheer weight of numbers. They bound him hand and foot, so he thought they must be human; what sort of humans, he had no idea.

At last they lifted him, half dragging and half pushing him out of the black chamber into an inner courtyard of the temple. Here he got a good look at his captors. There must have been a hundred of them—short, stocky men, with great beards that covered their faces and fell upon their hairy chests. They had long, thick matted hair, sloped foreheads, and short, heavy crooked legs. Around their loins they wore the skins of leopards and lions; around their necks he saw great necklaces made of the claws of these same animals. Massive circlets of gold adorned their arms and legs. For weapons they carried heavy, knotted clubs, and each carried a long, wicked-looking knife in his belt.

Most startlingly, they had white skin—at least where it could be seen beneath the dirt. They looked very evil. While they were obviously not dead, thought Tarzan, Busuli had not been so far from the truth.

They still had not spoken, but one of them gestured to the others. They then left him lying on the concrete floor while they trooped off into another part of the temple.

As Tarzan lay there on his back, he saw that the temple entirely surrounded the little enclosure, and that on all sides its lofty walls rose high above him. At the domed top a small patch of blue sky was visible, and, in one direction he could see foliage through an opening. Above where he lay, the walls were set with a series of open balconies, and now and then the captive glimpsed bright eyes gleaming from beneath masses of tumbling hair, peering down upon him from above.

The ape-man gently tested the bonds, and while they seemed breakable, he would wait until he was alone to put them to the crucial test.

He had lain tied up in the courtyard for several hours before the first rays of sunlight came through the opening atop the dome. Almost simultaneously, he heard the pattering of bare feet in the corridors around him, and a moment later saw the balconies above fill with crafty faces as twenty or more of the hairy men entered the courtyard.

For a moment every eye was bent up to the noonday sun, and then in unison the people in the galleries and the court below took up a low, weird chant. Presently, those around Tarzan began to dance to the solemn rhythm. They circled him slowly, like shuffling bears, keeping their eyes fixed upon the sun.

For ten minutes or more they kept up their chant and steps, and then suddenly, and in perfect unison, they turned toward their victim. With upraised clubs and fearful howls, their features contorted in savagery, they rushed upon him.

At the same instant a female figure dashed into the midst of the bloodthirsty horde. With a club like their own—except of made of gold—she beat back the advancing men.

CHAPTER 20

La, the High Priestess

For a moment Tarzan thought it was a miracle. The girl had single-handedly driven off twenty apelike males. When he saw them resume their dance about him while she chanted to them, he realized why he had been preserved. He was the central figure in a ceremony led by this priestess and her twenty priests.

After a moment or two the girl drew a knife, leaned over Tarzan and cut the bonds from his legs. Then, as the men stopped their dance and approached, she motioned him to rise. Placing the rope around his neck, she led him across the courtyard, the men following in twos. The procession went through winding corridors, deep into the temple, until they came to a large chamber with an altar in the center.

Then Tarzan understood: these were sun worshippers. His rescue by the priestess, with the sun looking down, was all part of the ritual. And from the brownish-red stains caking the stone altar and floor, and the many human skulls grinning from the walls, it was obvious why the woman had 'saved' him: to be sacrificed to their fiery god.

The priestess led the victim to the altar steps. Again the galleries above filled with watchers, while from an arched doorway a procession of women filed slowly in. Like the priests, these priestesses wore only animal skins belted about their waists, but their masses of black hair were held in place by a great deal of gold jewelry, with long strings of golden ornaments hanging from the sides. The females were a lot better looking than the males, with large, soft, intelligent-looking eyes and attractive features.

Each priestess carried two golden cups, and as they lined up along one side of the altar the men formed across from them, advancing and each taking a cup from the female opposite. Then the chant resumed, and presently, from a dark passageway beyond the altar, another woman emerged.

The high priestess, thought Tarzan. She was young, with a rather intelligent and shapely face. Her ornaments were similar to those of her assistants, but fancier. Her bare arms and legs were almost covered in jewelry, and she wore a leopard skin belted by a tight girdle of golden rings. From this girdle hung a long, jeweled knife, and in her hand was a slender wand.

As she advanced to the opposite side of the altar she halted and the chanting ceased. The priests and priestesses knelt before her. Extending her wand above them, she recited a long, repetitive prayer. Her voice was soft and musical—Tarzan could hardly picture its owner transformed by religious zeal into a wild-eyed executioner, who would probably be the first to drink her victim's warm blood from the golden cup on the altar.

As she finished her prayer, she looked Tarzan over for the first time—and with considerable interest. Then she addressed him, and stood waiting for a reply.

"I do not understand your language," said Tarzan. "Possibly we may speak together in another tongue?" But she could not understand him in French, English, Arabic, Waziri, or the West African dialect.

Shaking her head, she sounded weary in her voice as she motioned for the rites to continue. The priests now circled in a repetition of their dance, finally ended by a command from the high priestess. All the while, she had stood looking intently at Tarzan.

At her signal the men rushed upon the ape-man, lifted him up, and laid him on his back across the altar, his head hanging over one edge, his legs over the other. Then they and the women formed two lines, with their little golden cups ready to capture a share of the victim's lifeblood.

In the line of priests, a dispute arose as to who might go first. A burly, apelike brute was attempting to push a smaller man to second place, but the smaller one appealed to the high priestess. She coldly sent the larger man grumbling to the back of the line.

Then the priestess, standing above Tarzan, began some sort of incantation. She slowly raised her thin, sharp knife.

It seemed ages to the ape-man before it halted, high above his unprotected chest. Then it started slowly downward, and picked up speed. At the end of the line, Tarzan could still hear the humiliated priest's grumbling, and it was getting louder. A priestess nearby rebuked him sharply. The knife stopped for an instant within inches of Tarzan as the high priestess shot a look of displeasure at the disruptive man.

There was a sudden commotion in the back of the line, and Tarzan looked in time to see the burly priest leap upon the woman opposite him, bashing out her brains with a single blow of his heavy club. Then Tarzan saw something he had seen many times among males of the jungle, from the bull apes of his tribe to Tantor, the elephant. The priest went mad, and with his heavy weapon and teeth began to attack everyone nearby, screaming in frightful rage, bashing and biting. Through it all the priestess stood with knife poised above Tarzan, her eyes fixed in horror upon the maniac who was killing everyone in sight. Anyone who could flee did so.

Soon the room was emptied except for the casualties on the floor, the victim upon the altar, the high priestess, and the madman. The man's wild eyes fell upon the woman with a new and sudden lust. Slowly he crept toward her and spoke. To Tarzan's surprise, he understood the language. It was the last one he would have expected: the low guttural barking of the great apes, his own mother tongue. The woman replied in the same language.

He was threatening her. She was trying to reason with him, for it was quite evident that he was not obeying her orders. The brute was quite close now, creeping around the end of the altar with his claw-like hands extended toward her. The woman was too absorbed in her own danger to see Tarzan straining at his bonds. As the brute leaped past Tarzan to clutch his victim, the ape-man gave one superhuman wrench. The effort sent him rolling from the altar to the stone floor on the opposite side from the priestess; but as he sprang to his feet the thongs fell away. But he was now alone. The high priestess and the mad priest had disappeared.

And then a muffled scream came from the cavernous opening through which the priestess had entered the chamber shortly before. Forgetting both his own safety, and the new possibility of escape, Tarzan of the Apes answered the call of the woman in danger. With a short leap he was at the gaping entrance, and a moment later was running down a flight of ancient concrete steps—wherever they might lead.

The faint light that filtered in from above

showed a large, low-ceiled vault from which several doorways led off into inky darkness. But there was no need to explore, for in front of him lay the mad brute atop the high priestess, apelike fingers clutching frantically at her throat as she struggled to escape.

As Tarzan's heavy hand fell on his shoulder, the priest released his victim and turned on her would-be rescuer. With foaming lips and bared fangs, the mad sun-worshiper battled Tarzan with the tenfold strength of a maniac. So great was his bloodlust that he forgot the dagger at his belt, using only the weapons nature had given him.

With these muscles, claws and fangs he had no advantage at all over Tarzan. They both fell to the floor tearing and pounding at one another like bull apes, while the priestess stood flattened against the wall, watching the snapping beasts before her with wide, fascinated eyes. At last she saw the stranger close one mighty hand on the brutal priest's throat, force his head far back, and rain blow after blow upon the upturned face.

A moment later Tarzan took the dagger from the lifeless body, arose, and shook himself like a lion. He placed a foot upon the carcass and raised his head to give the victory cry of his kind, then thought better of it.

The woman now began to consider her probable fate. She had, after all, been about to kill Tarzan. She looked around to find a path of escape. The darkness of a corridor was near at hand, but as she turned to dart into it the ape-man's eyes fell upon her, and with a quick leap he was at her side, grasping her arm.

"Wait!" said Tarzan of the Apes, in the language of the tribe of Kerchak.

The girl looked at him in astonishment. "Who are you," she whispered, "who speaks the language of the first man?"

"I am Tarzan of the Apes," he answered.

"What do you want of me?" she continued. "Why did you save me from Tha?"

"I could not stand and watch a woman be murdered."

"But what will you do with me now?" she pressed.

"Nothing," he replied, "but you can do something for me. You can lead me out of this place to freedom." He had not the slightest hope she would, of course. The sacrificial ceremony would surely resume—but they would just as surely find an unbound, dagger-armed, Tarzan of the Apes a much harder target.

The woman stood looking at him for a long moment before she spoke.

"You are a very wonderful man," she said, "the sort of man I have dreamed of since I was a little girl—the kind my ancestors must have been. They built this mighty city so that they might mine its fabulous wealth. For this, they gave up their far-away civilization. I cannot understand why you rescued me in the first place, or why you do not want revenge upon me now. I nearly put you to death with my own hand."

"I presume," replied the ape-man, "that you were following your religion. I cannot blame you for that, though I also doubt I would want to convert to your beliefs. But who are you, and your people?"

"I am La, high priestess of the Temple of the Sun, in the city of Opar. We are descendants of a people who came here more than ten thousand years ago in search of gold. They were rich and powerful, and often went back and forth by sea between here and their native land far to the north. During the rainy season, this place was run by just a few, who kept their slaves busy mining the gold.

"One year the return of the main group was delayed. After weeks of waiting, our people sent a ship to search, but our ancient homeland had apparently sunk into the sea. That was the beginning of the downfall of my people. They soon fell victim to the greater numbers of the black tribes to north and south. One by one our cities were abandoned or taken, until our last remnant took shelter in this mighty mountain fortress.

"Since then we have slowly dwindled in every way. Now we are no better than a small tribe of savage apes. In fact, the apes have long lived with us; we call them the 'first men,' and their language is our normal speech. Only in rituals do we try to use our true mother tongue. Someday that will be forgotten, and we will speak only ape-language. Right now we still banish those of our people who take apes as mates, but when that custom of punishment is forgotten as well, we will have made our final descent back into beast-hood.

"But why are you more human than the others?" asked the man.

"For some reason, the women have not regressed as rapidly as the men. It may be because only the lower types of men—slave overseers, for example—remained here at the time of the great catastrophe. In contrast, the temples housed our noblest daughters. I have remained more human because, for countless ages, my foremothers have been high priestesses—the sacred office descends from mother to daughter. Our husbands are chosen from the noblest men in the land, the best of whom marries the high priestess."

"From what I saw of the gentlemen above," said Tarzan, with a grin, "there should be little trouble in choosing among them."

The girl looked at him sternly for a moment. "Do not be sacrilegious," she said. "They are very holy men—they are priests."

"Then there are others who are more handsome?" he asked.

"The others are all uglier than the priests," she replied.

Tarzan shuddered at her fate, for even in the dim light of the vault he was impressed by her beauty.

"But how about me?" he asked suddenly. "Are you going to lead me to liberty?"

"You have been chosen by The Flaming God as his own," she answered solemnly. "Not even I have the power to save you if they find you again, but I do not intend for them to get too close. You risked your life to save mine; I must do the same for you. It may take days, but in the end I think that I can lead you outside. Come! They will look here for me soon, and if they find us together they will assume that I have betrayed my god and kill us both."

"You must not take the risk, then," he said quickly. "I will return to the temple, and if I can fight my way to freedom you will not fall under suspicion."

"I will not allow it. Now follow me," she insisted. "We have already remained here too long to avoid suspicion. I will hide you, and then return alone. I will then tell them that I was long unconscious after you killed Tha, and that I do not know where you went."

And so she led him through winding, gloomy corridors, until finally they came to a small chamber lit by a little light filtered through a stone grating in the ceiling.

"This is the Chamber of the Dead," she said. "None will dare search for you here. I will return after it is dark, by which time I may have found a way for you to escape."

She was gone, and Tarzan of the Apes was left alone in the Chamber of the Dead, beneath the long-dead city of Opar.

CHAPTER 21

The Castaways

Clayton dreamed that he was drinking his fill of pure, delightful fresh water—and awoke to find himself being soaked by a heavy tropical shower.

He opened his mouth and drank, and soon had enough strength to raise himself up on his hands. Across his legs lay Monsieur Thuran. A few feet aft Jane Porter lay in a pitiful little heap, dead or nearly so.

Getting free of Thuran's weight, he crawled toward the girl and cradled her head in his arms. Refusing to abandon hope, he seized a water-soaked rag and squeezed the precious drops between the swollen lips of the girl who had so recently been a happy, youthful, glorious beauty.

For some time there was no reaction, but at last her eyelids moved. He rubbed the thin hands, and forced a few more drops of water into the parched throat. The girl opened her eyes, looking up at him for a long time before she regained awareness.

"Water?" she whispered. "Are we saved?"

"It is raining," he explained. "We can at least drink. Already it has revived us both."

"Monsieur Thuran?" she asked. "He did not kill you. Is he dead?"

"I do not know," replied Clayton. "If he lives and this rain revives him—" He stopped there, wishing not to add to the horrors she had already endured.

"Where is he?" she asked.

Clayton nodded his head toward the silent form of the Russian. For a time, neither one spoke.

"I will see if I can revive him," said Clayton at length.

"No," she whispered, grasping his arm. "He will kill you when the water has given him strength. If he is dying, let him die. Do not leave me alone in this boat with that beast."

Clayton hesitated. Honor demanded that he

attempt to revive Thuran, and there was the possibility—even the hope—that the Russian was beyond help. As he sat pondering this, he raised his eyes from Thuran's body and looked to the horizon. Then he staggered weakly to his feet with a little cry of joy.

"Land, Jane!" he croaked out. "Thank God, land!"

She looked, and not a hundred yards away, she saw a yellow beach. Beyond it was the luxuriant foliage of a tropical jungle.

"Now you may revive him," said Jane Porter, for she, too, had felt guilty. It took most of half an hour before the Russian could open his eyes, and by the time he understood their good fortune, the boat was gently washing ashore onto the sand.

Clayton found strength to stagger ashore with rope to tie up the boat. Next he made his way toward the nearby jungle. His former experience in the jungle had taught him what was edible, and after nearly an hour he returned with an armful of tropical fruit.

The rain had ceased, and the hot sun was beating down so mercilessly that Jane Porter insisted on coming ashore to find shade. The food and drink gave them just enough energy to reach the partial shade of a small tree, where they collapsed in exhaustion and slept until dark.

For a month they lived on the beach in comparative safety as their strength returned. The two men constructed a rude shelter in the branches of a tree, high enough from the ground to be safe from the larger beasts of prey. By day they gathered fruits and trapped small rodents; at night they lay nervously in the shelter while predators prowled the area. They slept on jungle grasses, and Clayton made a crude divider to give Jane some privacy. She slept covered by the old overcoat that Clayton had gone back for at the train station in Wisconsin.

From the first, the Russian showed his true character—selfish, arrogant, cowardly, and lustful. Twice he and Clayton fought over Thuran's attitude toward Jane. Clayton dared not leave her alone with him for an instant. The existence of the Englishman and his fiancée was a nightmare, and yet they lived on in hope of ultimate rescue.

Jane Porter often thought of her other experience on this wild shore. If the invincible forest god of that time were here now, there would be nothing to fear from either jungle beasts or from the bestial Thuran. She could not avoid comparing Clayton to Tarzan of the Apes; she knew what would have happened had Monsieur Thuran confronted the ape-man. Once, when Clayton was out getting water, and Thuran had said something crude to her, she voiced her thoughts.

"Be glad, Monsieur Thuran," she said, "that the poor Monsieur Tarzan who was lost at sea is not here now."

"You knew the pig?" asked Thuran, with a sneer.

"I knew the man," she replied. "The only real man, I think, that I have ever known."

The Russian sensed something beyond friendship in her tone of voice. Here was the opportunity for further revenge upon Tarzan's memory.

"He was worse than a pig," he cried. "He was a coward. He wronged a woman, and to save himself from her husband's righteous fury, he blamed it all on her. That failed, and the husband challenged him to a duel, so he fled France aboard that ship. I know because the wronged woman is my sister. And one more thing—your brave Monsieur Tarzan leaped overboard in fear because I recognized him, and demanded satisfaction from him the following morning. We could have fought with knives in my stateroom."

Jane Porter laughed. "No one who has known both Monsieur Tarzan and you could ever believe such an impossible tale."

"Then why did he travel under an assumed name?" asked Monsieur Thuran.

"I do not believe you," she cried, but nevertheless the seed of suspicion was sown, for she knew that Hazel Strong had known her forest god only as 'John Caldwell,' of London.

Unknown to them, barely five miles north was the snug cabin of Tarzan of the Apes. It might as well have been in France.

Farther up the coast—a few miles north of the cabin—lived a little party of eighteen in crude but well-built shelters, the occupants of the other three boats from the *Lady Alice*. In a smooth sea, they had rowed ashore in less than three days, avoiding all the worst horrors of the shipwreck. All of them hoped that the fourth boat had been quickly picked up and that a search of the coast would be made. Since all the firearms and ammunition on the yacht had been in Lord Tennington's boat, they were well equipped for hunting and defense.

Professor Archimedes Q. Porter was their only immediate worry. He had convinced himself that his daughter had been rescued by a passing steamer. With no need to worry about her, he devoted his great mind solely to the weighty scientific problems he considered appropriate to one of his learning.

"Never," said the exhausted Mr. Samuel T. Philander to Lord Tennington, "never has Professor Porter been more difficult—even impossible. Why, only this morning I let him out of my sight for but half an hour, and found him missing. And, bless me, sir, where do you imagine I discovered him? A half mile out in the ocean in one of the lifeboats, rowing away for dear life, in circles because he had only one oar. When one of the sailors took me out to him, and I suggested an immediate return to shore, he accused me of 'obstructing scientific progress.' Apparently he has made some arcane discovery relating to nebulas, and was rowing over to consult research materials in a private collection in New York City. Only with the greatest difficulty did I persuade him to return to shore without having to resort to force," concluded Mr. Philander.

Miss Strong and her mother bore up very bravely. They were not as ready as the others to assume that the other three castaways had been picked up safely. Esmeralda was often in tears at the cruel fate that had separated her from her "poor li'l honey." Lord Tennington remained the big-hearted host, always seeking his guests' comfort, and his leadership remained firm, calm and intelligent.

If this relatively secure party of castaways had seen the ragged, frightened trio a few miles south of them, they would barely have recognized them. Clayton and Monsieur Thuran were almost naked, their clothes badly torn by the thorns and tangles of the jungle as they foraged for food. Jane was only marginally better off. Clayton had saved all the small rodent pelts, and had stretched and scraped them; soon he fashioned a crude sort of sleeveless tunic out of them using grasses and animal tendons. It looked comical and smelled awful. When decency forced him to put it on, not even the misery of their condition could prevent Jane from laughing heartily at sight of him.

Later, Thuran found it necessary to dress likewise. With their bare legs and unshaven faces, they looked like two prehistoric men. Thuran acted like one.

Nearly two months had passed when the first disaster occurred. It was prefaced by an adventure which nearly ended the sufferings of two of them for good.

Thuran, down with a fever, lay resting in the tree. Clayton had gone into the jungle in search of food. As he returned, Jane Porter walked to meet him.

Behind Clayton, cunning and crafty, crept an old and mangy lion. He had not eaten for three days, and months of increasing hunger had brought him far afield in search of easier prey. At last he had found nature's weakest prey. Old Numa would shortly dine.

Unaware of the lurking death behind him, Clayton strode out into the open toward Jane. He had reached her side, a hundred feet from the edge of the jungle, when beyond him the woman saw the tawny head part the grasses. The huge beast crept softly into view.

Jane was too terrified to cry out, but her fear-widened eyes alerted Clayton. A quick glance behind him revealed a hopeless situation. The lion was barely thirty paces from them, and they were that far from the shelter. The man was armed with no more than a stout stick—it might as well have been a toy pop-gun. Hungry old Numa opened his huge jaws and vented months of starved rage in a series of deafening roars that made the ground tremble.

"Run, Jane!" cried Clayton. "Quick! Run for the shelter!" But her paralyzed muscles refused to respond, and she stood silently fixated on the advancing lion.

At the sound of that awful roar, Thuran had come to the opening of the shelter. When he saw the situation he hopped up and down, shrieking to them in Russian:

"Run! Run!" he cried. "Run, or I shall be left all alone in this horrible place," and then he broke down and wept. For a moment this new voice distracted old Numa, who halted to glance curiously toward the tree.

The months of strain and hardship finally, truly, hit Clayton like a great weight dropped upon him. He could endure it all no longer. Turning his back on the beast, he buried his head in his arms and waited.

The girl looked at him in horror. Why did he not do something? If he must die, why not die like a man—even if it meant futilely beating at that terrible face with his puny stick? Tarzan of the Apes, at least, would have gone down fighting to the death.

Now Numa was crouching to spring. Jane Porter sank to her knees in prayer, closing her eyes to shut out the last hideous instant. Thuran fainted.

Seconds dragged into minutes, and yet the beast did not spring. Clayton was trembling in fright—a moment more and he would collapse.

Jane Porter could endure it no longer. She opened her eyes. Could she be dreaming?

"William," she whispered, "look!"

Clayton raised his head and turned toward the lion, and cried out in surprise. At their very feet the beast lay crumpled in death. A heavy African spear protruded from the tawny hide, having entered above the right shoulder and pierced all the way through to the heart.

Jane staggered weakly to her feet. Clayton put out his arms to steady her, and then drew her close. Pressing her head against his shoulder, he bent to kiss her in thanksgiving.

Gently she pushed him away.

"Please do not do that, William," she said. "The past brief moments have made me realize something. I do not wish to hurt you, but I can no longer keep an impulsive promise I made to you. I can deceive myself no longer: I cannot marry you, William, should we ever get back to civilization."

"Why, Jane," he cried, "what do you mean? How can our rescue have altered your feelings toward me? You are suffering from nerves— tomorrow you will be yourself again."

"I am more myself this minute than I have been for over a year," she replied. "I have been forcibly reminded that the bravest man that ever lived honored me with his love. Until it was too late I did not realize that I loved him too, and so I sent him away. He is dead now, and I shall never marry. I certainly could not wed a lesser man without comparing his courage to that of the one I love—and finding it lacking. Do you understand me?"

"Yes," he answered, with bowed head, his face flushing with shame.

On the next day came the great calamity.

CHAPTER 22

The Treasure Vaults of Opar

It was quite dark before La, the high priestess, returned to the Chamber of the Dead with food and drink for Tarzan. He came out to meet her.

"They are furious," said she. "Never before has a human sacrifice escaped the altar. Already fifty of them are looking for you. They have searched the whole temple—except this single room."

"Why do they fear to come here?" he asked.

"It is the Chamber of the Dead. Here the dead return to worship. On this ancient altar the dead sacrifice the living—if they find a victim here. Our people shun this chamber for that reason."

"But you?" he asked.

"I am high priestess. I occasionally bring them a human sacrifice. Only I may safely enter here."

"Why have the dead not seized me?" he asked, humoring her grotesque belief.

She looked at him quizzically for a moment, then replied:

"It is the duty of a high priestess to instruct and interpret, according to the creed laid down in the past, but the creed does not require her to believe. The more one knows of one's religion, the less one believes. No one living knows more of my religion than I do."

"Then your only fear in helping me escape is that your people may discover your deception?"

"Yes. The dead are dead; they cannot harm or help. We must depend entirely upon ourselves, and the sooner we act, the better. It was dangerous to bring you food, and if I keep doing so, I will be caught. Come, let us see how far we are able to travel toward liberty before I must return."

She led him back to the chamber beneath the altar room, then turned into one of the branching corridors. For ten minutes they groped along until they came to a closed door. He heard her fumbling with a key, and soon he heard a metal bolt moving. The door squeaked open, and they entered.

"You will be safe here until tomorrow night," she said. Then she went out, closed the door, and locked it behind her.

It was too dark to see. Cautiously he felt forward until he touched a wall, then very slowly he traveled around the four walls of the chamber. Apparently it was about twenty feet square, with a concrete floor and walls made of granite stones laid together without mortar.

The first time around the walls Tarzan felt something quite unexpected: a faint breeze. Circling the room again, he isolated the spot. Sure enough, fresh air was blowing through the masonry here. He tested the wall, and found a stone he could easily lift out. Soon he had removed a dozen, and reached in to check for further layers of granite stones.

To his surprise, he felt nothing but space beyond the opening. In a few minutes he removed enough of the wall to squeeze through. Once on the other side, he thought he saw a faint glow ahead. He crawled cautiously forward, but after about fifteen feet the floor dropped away. He could not feel any bottom to the hole, nor could he reach to the other side. Then suddenly there was a flood of soft, silvery light. He looked up to see a round opening with a patch of starry sky and a small part of the moon. Now he could see that the hole was about fifteen feet wide, and far below was a shimmer of water. A well! But what did this well have to do with the dungeon?

Across the well, Tarzan saw another opening in the opposite wall. Could it lead to an escape route? He would investigate. First he went back, got the stones he had removed, and replaced them from the well side of the wall. The dust on the blocks made it clear that the passage had not been used for years. Then Tarzan leaped easily across the well, and soon he was moving cautiously along a narrow tunnel.

Some hundred feet later, he came to a flight of steps leading downward. Twenty feet below, the steps leveled off to a passage ending at a heavy wooden door secured by massive, dusty wooden bars. His hopes rose: either this led to a prison, or the bars were meant to keep the outside world out. It could lead to freedom! As he pushed the massive door aside, its great hinges shrieked in protest. For a moment Tarzan paused to listen for any sounds of activity above. Hearing nothing, he advanced beyond the doorway.

Feeling his way carefully, he found himself in a large chamber, the walls and floor of which were stacked with metal ingots. They were all of the same strange bricklike size and shape. They could surely not be gold; this was too much wealth to imagine. They must be of some baser metal, he thought. He grabbed one to take along and found it was heavy as lead.

At the far end of the chamber he opened another barred door to reveal a long, straight passage. Tarzan figured he was already beyond the outer walls of the temple. If he only knew which way! If westward, then he must also be beyond the city's outer walls. He forged rapidly ahead for half an hour and then came to another flight of steps leading upward. The steps began in concrete, then gave way to granite and began to spiral upward. One final turn, and above him shone the starry sky! Tarzan hastened up a steep incline, and came out on the rough top of a granite boulder the size of a building.

A mile away lay the ruined city of Opar, its domes and turrets bathed in the soft light of the African moon. Tarzan dropped his eyes to the ingot he had brought—the moon's bright light showed it to be pure gold. Then he gazed upon the ancient piles of crumbling grandeur in the distance.

"Opar," he mused, "enchanted city of a dead and forgotten past. City of beauties and beasts; deadly horrors and fabulous riches."

The boulder lay well out in the plain between the city and the distant cliffs he and his Waziri warriors had scaled the morning before. At considerable peril, he descended the rough face of the huge stone and soon stood on the soft soil of the valley. Without a backward glance at Opar, he set off at a rapid trot across the valley.

The sun was just rising as he crested the flat mountain at the valley's western boundary. Far beneath him he saw smoke rising above the treetops at the base of the foothills. Men, obviously; could it be the ones sent to track him down?

Swiftly he climbed down the cliff, then dropped into a narrow ravine which led down to the forest and hastened toward the smoke. When he reached the trees, he took to them and advanced the remaining quarter mile cautiously until he came in sight of a *boma* with many fires. Safe inside the walls sat his fifty Waziri. He called to them in their own tongue:

"Arise, my warriors, and greet your king!"

With exclamations of surprise and fear the warriors leaped to their feet, reaching for weapons. Then Tarzan dropped lightly from an overhanging branch into their midst. When they realized that it was indeed their chief in the flesh, they went mad with joy.

"We were afraid, oh Waziri," cried Busuli. "We are ashamed that we left you to explore alone; but we soon swore to return and save you, or at least avenge you. We were just preparing to scale the heights once more and cross the valley to the terrible city."

"Have you seen fifty ugly men pass down from the cliffs into this forest, my warriors?" asked Tarzan.

"Yes, Waziri," replied Busuli. "They passed us late yesterday, as we were about to turn back after you. We heard them coming from far away, and withdrew into the forest to let them pass. They were waddling rapidly along on their short legs, and some went on all fours like Bolgani, the gorilla. They were primitive, Waziri."

When Tarzan had told the whole story, all agreed to his plan to return by night and bring away all the treasure they could carry. So, as dusk fell across the desolate valley of Opar, fifty African warriors set forth at a smart trot. They again scaled the cliffs, and soon stood at the foot of the giant boulder that loomed before the city.

It was much harder to get fifty warriors up the face of the boulder than it had been to get himself down, but Tarzan finally found enough tiny footholds to ascend it. Fortunately, his warriors had brought rope, and with this Tarzan hoisted them up one by one to the top of the boulder. Immediately Tarzan led them to the treasure chamber, where each was given two ingots to carry—about eighty pounds apiece.

By midnight the entire party stood once more at the foot of the boulder, but with their heavy loads it was mid-morning before they reached the summit of the cliffs. From there the homeward journey was slow; the proud fighting men were unused to serving as porters. But they bore their burdens with no complaints, and at the end of thirty days entered their own country.

Here, instead of continuing northwest toward their village, Tarzan guided them almost directly west. On the morning of the thirty-third day, he ordered them to break camp and return to their own village, leaving the gold where they had stacked it the previous night.

"And you, Waziri?" they asked.

"I shall remain here for a few days, my warriors," he replied. "Now hasten back to your wives and children."

When they had gone, Tarzan gathered up two of the ingots and sprang into a tree. He traveled lightly above the undergrowth for a couple of hundred yards, to emerge suddenly upon a circular clearing girdled by giant trees. In the center of this natural amphitheater was a little flat-topped mound of hard earth.

Tarzan had been to this secluded spot hundreds of times. It was so densely surrounded by thorn bushes and tangled vines that not even Sheeta, the leopard, could worm his way within, nor could Tantor's giant strength force a way in. The council chamber of the great apes was safe from nearly all of the deadlier dwellers of the jungle.

It took him fifty more trips to transfer all the ingots into the amphitheater. Then from the hollow of an ancient, lightning-blasted tree he produced the very shovel he had once used to uncover the chest of Professor Archimedes Q. Porter. He dug a long trench and buried the fortune brought from the forgotten treasure vaults of Opar.

That night he slept in the amphitheater, and early the next morning set out to revisit his cabin before returning to his Waziri. Finding things as he had left them, he went forth into the jungle to hunt, intending to feast and sleep in comfort the coming night. He roamed five miles south, toward the banks of a fair-sized river that entered the sea about six miles from his cabin. He had gone inland about half a mile when suddenly his sensitive nostrils picked up the scent that sets the whole jungle aquiver.

Man.

The wind was blowing off the ocean, so Tarzan knew that people were west of him. Mixed with the man-scent was the scent of Numa. He had better hasten, he thought. Numa might be hunting.

When he came through the trees to the edge of the jungle he saw a white woman kneeling in prayer. Before her stood a primitive white man, his face buried in his arms. He could not see their faces. Behind the man advanced mangy old Numa.

There was not a second to spare; no time to ready his bow, nor to charge with the knife. There was but a single hope—and with the quickness of thought the ape-man acted.

A brawny arm went back and then shot his spear forward. Swift death tore through the leaves to bury itself in the heart of the crouching lion. Without a sound he rolled over at the very feet of his intended victims—dead. For a moment neither the man nor the woman moved. Then the latter opened her eyes to look with wonder at the dead beast.

As that beautiful head went up Tarzan of the Apes gasped in astonishment. Was he mad? It could not be the woman he loved! But, indeed, it was none other.

The woman rose, and the man took her in his arms to kiss her.

The ape-man saw red through a bloody mist of murder, and the old scar upon his forehead burned scarlet against his brown hide. In fury he fitted a poisoned shaft to his bow. An ugly light gleamed in those gray eyes as he sighted on the back of the unsuspecting man beneath him.

For an instant he glanced along the finely-crafted shaft, drawing the bowstring far back, so that the arrow might be driven through his rival's heart.

But he did not release it. Slowly the point of the arrow drooped; the scar upon the brown forehead faded; the bowstring relaxed; and Tarzan of the Apes, with bowed head, turned sadly into the jungle toward the village of the Waziri.

CHAPTER 23

The Fifty Frightful Men

For several long minutes Jane Porter and William Clayton stood silently looking at the spear-impaled corpse of the lion.

"Who could it have been?" she whispered.

"God knows!" replied Clayton.

"If it is a friend, why does he not show himself?" continued Jane. "Should we not at least call out to him in thanks?"

Clayton mechanically did so, but there was no response.

Jane Porter shuddered. "The mysterious jungle," she murmured.

"We had best return to the shelter," said Clayton. "You will be safer there. I am no protection whatever," he added bitterly.

"Do not say that, William," she urged, deeply sorry for having hurt him. "You have done your best. You have been noble and brave, but you are no superman—I know of only one man who could have done more. I did not wish to wound you, just to be clear once and for all that I cannot marry you."

"I think I understand," he replied. "Let us speak no more of it until we return to civilization."

The next day Thuran sank into a fevered, raving delirium. Neither Jane nor Clayton was eager to help him; a part of Clayton even wished for Thuran's death. In case anything were to happen to him, he reasoned, Jane would be far safer without Thuran than with him.

The Englishman had retrieved the heavy spear from the lion. When he went hunting in the forest that morning, the weapon made him feel safer, and he went deeper into the jungle this time.

To escape from the ravings of the fevered Russian, Jane Porter had climbed down from the tree, but she dared not venture farther. Sitting beside the crude ladder Clayton had built, she watched the sea in hopes of sighting a vessel.

With her back to the jungle, she did not see the savage face that peered from between the grasses. Little bloodshot eyes scanned her and the beach intently. Presently another head appeared, and then another and another. Thuran began to rave again, and the heads disappeared as silently and as suddenly as they had come. When the woman showed no concern at the continued wailing, the heads soon poked out again.

One by one, ugly forms began to stalk the unsuspecting woman. A faint rustling of the grasses alerted her; she turned, gave a little shriek of fear, and got to her feet. Then they rushed her, and one of the creatures lifted her in long, gorilla-like arms and carried her into the jungle, stifling her screams with a filthy, hairy paw. The shock was too much for nerves weakened by hardship, and she lost consciousness.

When she regained her senses, she found herself lying in a little clearing, at night, somewhere in the forest. A huge fire burned brightly. Around it squatted fifty frightful men with hairy heads and faces, long arms and crooked legs.

They gnawed like beasts on filthy-looking food. A pot boiled at the fire, and now and then one of them would stab into it with a sharp stick and drag out a hunk of meat. When they discovered that their captive was awake, a piece of this repulsive stew was tossed to her from the foul hand of a nearby diner. She refused to touch it, and closed her eyes as a wave of nausea hit.

For many days they traveled through the dense forest. The exhausted woman was half dragged, half pushed through the long, hot, tedious days. Occasionally she would stumble and fall, but they cuffed and kicked her back to her feet. Soon, her shoes wore out completely and were discarded. Her clothes were torn to tatters, showing where her once pale and tender skin was raw and bleeding from thorns and brambles.

Near the end of the journey, she was too exhausted to move. They hit and kicked her harder, and spoke in threatening tones, but all she did was lay there and hope for a death that did not come. At last the frightful men figured out that she was no longer able to walk on her bloodied feet, so they picked her up to carry her the rest of the way.

Late one afternoon she saw the ruined walls of a mighty city looming before them, but she was too weak and sick to care. Wherever it was, she was sure she would die there.

At last they passed through a crack in the wall and came into the ruined city within. They took her inside a crumbling building, and here there were hundreds more of the same creatures who had brought her—but there were also females, who looked less horrible. Her hopes of relief were quickly dashed, however, when the women offered her no sympathy at all. At least they did not join in her mistreatment.

After everyone had gotten a good look at her, Jane was carried to a dark underground chamber. She was left there on the bare floor, with metal bowls of water and food.

For a week she saw only the women who brought her food and water. Her strength was slowly returning. Soon she would be a fitting sacrifice to The Flaming God. Fortunately, she had no idea of this god—or his rites.

As Tarzan of the Apes moved slowly through the jungle after saving Clayton and Jane Porter from the fangs of Numa, his mind was filled with all the sorrow of a twice-broken heart. He was glad that he had not killed Clayton. He had been overcome with a moment's rage and, for a second, the fierce jungle code had taken over. Then the softer sentiments of chivalry had risen above the fires of his passion, saving him from committing murder. Many times he gave thanks that these feelings had triumphed before he had released the polished, poisoned arrow.

He could not stand the idea of returning to the Waziri. It was nothing they had or had not done, but because he had no further wish for any human contact. He would range alone through the jungle for a time until the pain of his heart dulled.

That night he slept again in the amphitheater of the apes, and for several days he hunted from there, returning at night. On the afternoon of the third day he returned early to rest. He had only napped for a few moments when he heard a familiar sound, far away: the passing of a band of great apes. He listened carefully for several minutes— they were coming closer.

Tarzan arose and stretched, his keen ears following their movements. Presently he caught their scent. As they came closer to the amphitheater, Tarzan of the Apes melted into the branches on the other side of the arena to watch the newcomers. He had not long to wait.

A fierce, hairy face appeared among the lower branches opposite him. The cruel little eyes inspected the clearing and then gave a chattered report to those behind. Tarzan understood: the scout was telling the others that the coast was clear.

First the leader dropped lightly onto the soft carpet of the grassy floor, and then, one by one, nearly a hundred apes followed him. There were huge adults and several young. A few nursing babes clung close to the shaggy necks of their savage mothers.

Tarzan recognized many members of the tribe, for it was the one in which he had been raised. As little apes, many of the adults had been his boyhood playmates in this very jungle. He wondered if they would remember him, for apes tend to have short memories.

From their talk he learned that they had come to choose a new king. The previous one had fallen to his death from a broken limb.

Tarzan walked to the end of an overhanging limb in plain view of them. The quick eyes of a female saw him first, and she barked out to the others. Several huge bulls stood up to get a better view of the intruder. With bared fangs and bristling necks they advanced slowly toward him, growling.

"Karnath, I am Tarzan of the Apes," said the ape-man in the ape-tongue. "You remember me. We were little apes together. Together we teased Numa by throwing sticks and nuts at him from the safety of high branches."

The brute he had addressed stopped with a look of dull wonder on his savage face.

"And Magor," continued Tarzan, addressing another, "do you not recall your former king—he who slew the mighty Kerchak? Look at me! Am I not the same Tarzan—mighty hunter—that you all knew?"

The apes all crowded forward, now curious. They muttered among themselves for a few moments.

"What do you want among us now?" asked Karnath.

"Only peace," answered the ape-man.

Again the apes conferred. At length Karnath spoke again.

"Come in peace, then, Tarzan of the Apes," he said.

And so Tarzan of the Apes dropped lightly to the turf into the midst of the fierce horde. He had completed the cycle. He had returned to be, once again, a brute among brutes.

There were no extended greetings of the sort humans would have shared after a two-year separation. Most of the apes went about their activities, paying him no further attention.

One or two young bulls, too young to remember him, sidled up on all fours to sniff at him. One bared his fangs and growled threateningly. Had Tarzan backed off, the young bull would probably have been satisfied, but it would have assigned Tarzan lower status.

But Tarzan of the Apes did not back off. Instead, he swung his giant palm with all his might, catching the young bull alongside the head and sending him sprawling across the turf. The ape was up and at him again in a second, and this time they closed with tearing fingers and rending fangs—or so, at least, the young bull had intended. As it was, they had barely hit the ground when the ape-man's fingers tightened around his opponent's throat.

Soon the young bull ceased to struggle. When he lay quite still, Tarzan released his hold and arose. He did not wish to kill, only to teach a lesson: Tarzan of the Apes was still master.

The lesson was learned. Male apes of all ages kept out of his way. For several days the she-apes with young remained suspicious of him, and when he ventured too near, rushed upon him with furious roars. Tarzan would discreetly skip out of harm's way, for among the apes, no one but a mad bull will attack a mother. But after a while even the mothers became accustomed to him.

He hunted with them as he had long ago, and when they found that his superior intelligence— and his rope—enabled them to eat better, they began to look up to him as before. By the time they left the amphitheater to wander, he had been chosen again as their leader again.

The ape-man felt quite contented, if not happy. He could never be happy again, but he could at least be as far as possible from any reminders of his past misery. He had long ago given up any notion of returning to civilization; now he decided to forsake his African friends, the Waziri. He had started life as an ape—as an ape he would die.

He might indeed escape civilization, but he could not escape the fact that the woman he loved was both nearby and unsafe. Clayton obviously was not able to protect her. The more Tarzan thought of it, the more it bothered him. Eventually he grew angry with himself for placing his own selfish sorrow and jealousy above Jane Porter's safety.

The guilt continued to nag at his heart, until one day he had nearly decided to return to the coast to stand guard over Jane Porter and Clayton. Then came news that shattered those plans and sent him on a mad, death-defying dash to the east.

Among the apes, a young bull who cannot find a mate from his own tribe often goes forth to find one from another group. One such bull now returned with his new bride, and was telling of his adventures. Among other things, he told of seeing a great tribe of strange-looking apes.

"They were all hairy-faced bulls but one," he said, "and that one was a she, lighter in color even than this stranger," and he pointed at Tarzan.

The ape-man was all attention. He asked rapid-fire questions:

"Were the bulls short, with crooked legs?"

"They were."

"Did they wear the skins of Numa and Sheeta around their loins, and carry sticks and knives?"

"They did."

"And were there many yellow rings about their arms and legs?"

"Yes."

"And the she—was she small and slender, with light skin?"

"Yes."

"Did she seem to be one of the tribe, or was she a prisoner?"

"They dragged her along—sometimes by an arm—sometimes by the long fur that grew upon her head. They kicked and beat her; it was great fun to watch them."

"God!" muttered Tarzan.

"Where did you see them, and which way were they going?" continued the ape-man.

"They were beside the second water back there," and he pointed to the south. "When they passed me they were going upward along the edge of the water."

"When was this?" asked Tarzan.

"Half a moon since."

Without another word the ape-man sprang into the trees and fled like a spirit eastward in the direction of the forgotten city of Opar.

CHAPTER 24

How Tarzan Came Again to Opar

When Clayton returned to the shelter and found Jane Porter missing, he became frantic with fear and grief. The fever had left Monsieur Thuran quite suddenly, as sometimes happens, but the Russian was still weak and exhausted.

"Jane has vanished!" exclaimed Clayton. "Have you seen her?"

"I have heard nothing unusual," he said. "But then I have been unconscious much of the time."

Clayton would not have believed Thuran, except for his obvious weakness. In his present condition, the Russian could not even climb up and down the shelter's crude ladder, much less have harmed Jane. The Englishman searched the nearby jungle for traces until dark. He crossed the kidnappers' trail perhaps twenty times, but what would have been obvious to any jungle dweller was invisible to him.

As he searched, Clayton called out to Jane; this only succeeded in attracting Numa, the lion. Fortunately, he saw the shadowy form approaching in time to take refuge in a tree. The lion paced restlessly beneath him until dark. Even after Numa had left, Clayton dared not climb down, and he spent a terrifying night in the tree. The next morning he returned to the beach, all hope of finding Jane gone.

During the week that followed, Monsieur Thuran rapidly regained his strength, lying in the shelter while Clayton hunted food for both. Clayton moved to what had been Jane's side of the shelter; the men only had contact when Clayton brought the Russian food and water.

When Thuran was again able to hunt, Clayton caught the fever. For days he lay mostly delirious, but not once did the Russian come near him. He could not have held down food, but the craving for water was torture. In between attacks of delirium, he managed to make his way to the brook once per day to drink while Thuran enjoyed watching him suffer.

At last Clayton became too weak to climb down from the shelter. When he could endure the thirst no longer, he asked Thuran to fetch him a drink. The Russian went and got a dish of water, then stood at the partition with a nasty grin on his face.

"Here is water," he said. "But first let me remind you that you insulted me in front of the girl. You kept her to yourself, and would not share her with me—"

Clayton interrupted him. "Stop! What manner of dog are you, to insult the memory of a good woman! God! I was a fool ever to let you live."

"Here is all the water you will get," said the Russian, and he raised the basin to his lips and drank. He threw what was left out on the ground below, then turned and left the sick man.

Clayton rolled over, buried his face in his arms and gave up the battle.

The next day Thuran determined to set out northward along the coast in hopes of finding a settlement. He could be no worse off than he was here, and the dying Englishman's ravings were getting on his nerves, so he stole Clayton's spear and set forth. He thought of killing the sick man before he left, but decided that would be too merciful.

That same day he came to a little cabin by the beach. His hopes rose; it must surely be the outpost of a nearby settlement. Had he realized whose cabin it was, and how near that owner was, Nikolai Rokoff would have fled the place as he would the plague. Unaware, he remained for a few days in the secure comfort of the cabin before resuming his northward journey.

In Lord Tennington's camp, they were preparing to build better shelter, and then to send an expedition northward in search of relief. They had begun to doubt that the others had been rescued. No one spoke of it to Professor Porter, who was completely out of touch with reality.

Occasionally he would remark that a steamer should soon drop anchor offshore, or that the train might have been delayed by snowstorms.

"If I didn't know the dear old fellow so well by now," Tennington remarked to Miss Strong, "I would be quite certain that he was—er—not quite right."

"It would be funny if it were not so sad," she said. "I have known him all my life. He worships Jane, but others may not see this. The poor dear cannot conceive of death unless certain proof of it is thrust upon him."

"You'd never guess what he was doing yesterday," continued Tennington. "I was returning from a hunt when I met him walking rapidly along the game trail. His hands were clasped behind his back, and he was intent on the ground—probably headed to his death had I not intercepted him.

"'Why, where in the world are you going, professor?' I asked him. 'I am going into town, Lord Tennington,' he said, quite seriously, 'to complain to the postmaster about their delivery service. Why, sir, I haven't had a piece of mail in weeks. There should be several letters for me from Jane. The matter must be reported to Washington at once.'

"And would you believe it, Miss Strong," continued Tennington, "I had a terrible time convincing the old fellow that there was not only no postal service, but no town, and that Washington was on another continent. When he did realize, he began worrying about his daughter. I think it is the first time that he has really grasped our situation, or the likelihood that Miss Porter has not been rescued."

"I hate to think about it," said the girl, "and yet I can think of nothing else but those who are missing."

"Let us hope for the best," replied Tennington. "You yourself have been a splendid example of bravery, for in a way, your loss has been the greatest."

"Yes," she replied. "I loved Jane Porter as my own sister."

Tennington did not show his surprise, for that was not what he had meant. He had spent much time with this fair daughter of Maryland, and in one way, his fondness for her had put him in a dilemma. Monsieur Thuran had confided in him about their engagement, and now Tennington wondered increasingly whether that had been true. Miss Strong certainly showed no sign that it might be.

"And Monsieur Thuran, of course," said he. "If he were lost, you would surely be grieved."

She looked up at him quickly. "Monsieur Thuran had become a very dear friend," she said. "I liked him very much, though I have known him but a short time."

"Then you were not engaged to marry him?" he blurted out.

"Heavens, no!" she cried. "I did not care for him at all in that way."

Lord Tennington wanted to say something else to Hazel Strong, but somehow the words stuck in his throat. He started lamely, cleared his throat, hesitated, and ended by making some comment about the cabins and the upcoming rainy season. What he did not know was that she had gotten his message, and that she was now happier than she had ever been in her life.

Further conversation was interrupted by the sight of a strange-looking figure emerging from the jungle just south of the camp. The Englishman reached for his revolver, but when the half-naked, bearded creature called his name aloud and came running toward them, he dropped his hand and advanced to meet it.

None would have recognized this filthy, skeletal creature, covered by a single garment of small skins, as the well-dressed Monsieur Thuran from the *Lady Alice*. Before the rest learned of his presence, Tennington and Miss Strong asked him about his five boatmates.

"They are all dead," replied Thuran. "The three sailors died before we made land. Miss Porter was carried off into the jungle by some wild animal while I was stricken with fever. Clayton died of the same fever a few days ago. And to think that all this time we have been separated by but a few miles—how terrible!"

How long Jane Porter lay in the dark vault beneath the temple in the ancient city of Opar she did not know. She was delirious with fever for a time, but the illness passed and she began to regain her strength. A woman brought her food and drink every day, and watched her carefully. Eventually Jane was able to rise to her feet, which interested her captors, for the important day was approaching.

When it came, a young woman whom Jane had not seen before came with several others, and performed some sort of religious ceremony. Jane rejoiced, for surely a religious people would treat her humanely. Thus, when they led her from her dungeon through long, dark corridors, and up into a brilliant courtyard, she went willingly, for was she not among the servants of God? Even if they thought of God differently than she did, if they were godly people, they must be kind and good.

But when she saw a stone altar in the center of the courtyard, with dark brown stains leading from it to the nearby floor, she began to doubt. As they bound her ankles, and secured her wrists behind her, her doubts became fear. When she was laid across the altar, fear gave way to pure fright.

During the grotesque dance of the priests and priestesses that followed, she lay frozen in horror. She did not need to see the thin blade rising slowly above her to understand her impending fate. As the hand began its descent, Jane Porter closed her eyes and sent up a silent prayer to the Maker she was so soon to face, and fainted.

Tarzan of the Apes raced through the jungle toward the ruined city. It had taken his captors nearly a week to get there, but it took him only a day and a night to cover the distance. The young bull ape's story had convinced him, for there was not another small white "she" in all the jungle. The "bulls" had obviously been the grotesque excuses for manhood found in Opar. He could plainly picture Jane's fate: her dear, frail body would eventually lie across that altar.

But finally, after what seemed ages, he topped the barrier cliffs and looked down upon the ruins of dreadful Opar. He set off at a rapid trot across the dry, rocky ground. Would he be in time? If not, he would have revenge: he would be glad to wipe out the entire population of the terrible city.

It was nearly noon when he reached the great boulder. He scaled the huge granite stone like a cat, and a moment later he was running along the long, straight tunnel leading to the treasure vault. Soon he was at the edge of the well, looking across in the dim light at the wall he had dismantled and rebuilt.

As he paused, he heard faint sounds from above. His quick ears translated it: the dance of death before a sacrifice, and the singsong ritual of the high priestess. Could it be that the ceremony was now underway? After all this, was he to be a moment too late?

Like a deer he leaped across the narrow opening. He tore apart the stones and forced a small opening, then rammed his body through, bringing the rest of the wall crashing down. He did not care about the noise, and with a single leap he crossed the chamber and threw himself against the ancient door—and here he stopped. Not even his muscles could defeat the mighty bars on the other side.

There seemed but one option: to go all the way back to the boulder, and then come back the way he had first come into Opar with his Waziri warriors. If Jane truly lay upon the sacrificial altar at this moment, he would be too late to save her, but he must try anyway. Back he raced through the ruin of the wall.

At the well he heard again the litany of the high priestess, and glanced up at the opening twenty feet above. In his mad urgency to reach the inner courtyard that was so near, he was tempted to leap for it. If only he could get one end of his rope secured at the top of the skylight . . . then he had an idea!

Turning back to the tumbled wall, he seized one of the large, flat slabs from it. Hastily tying one end of his rope to the stone, he returned to the edge of the well and coiled the rope on the floor. Then he took the heavy slab in both hands, swung it several times, and let the weight fly up at a slight angle. Sure enough, it grazed the far edge and tumbled over into the court beyond.

Tarzan pulled on the rope until he felt that the stone was well wedged, and then he swung out over the black depths of the well. He immediately felt the rope slip from above. He waited there in awful suspense as it dropped in little jerks, inch by inch. Would the stone catch at the very edge, or would his weight drag it over to fall upon him as he hurtled into the unknown depths below?

CHAPTER 25

Through the Forest Primeval

For a brief, sickening moment, Tarzan felt the rope slipping, and heard the block of stone scraping against the masonry above. Then the rope halted—the stone had caught at the very edge! Gingerly the ape-man clambered up, and soon his head was above the edge of the skylight. He vaulted up into the empty courtyard.

Tarzan could hear the voice of La, the high priestess, from the nearby temple. The sounds of dance had ceased. It must be almost time for the knife to fall, he thought, as he ran rapidly toward the sound of the her voice.

He came to the doorway of the great roofless chamber. Between him and the altar was the long row of priests and priestesses, waiting with their golden cups for the warm blood. La's hand was descending slowly toward the chest of the frail, quiet figure stretched out on the hard stone.

Tarzan gasped, almost sobbed, as he recognized the features of the woman he loved. And then the scar on his forehead flamed to scarlet, a red mist floated before his eyes, and, with the awful roar of the bull ape gone mad, he sprang like a huge lion into the midst of it all.

Seizing a club from the nearest priest, he bashed his way toward the altar like a demon. The hand of La had paused at the interruption; now she went pale. She had never been able to figure out how the strange man had escaped. She had never intended this attractive man to leave Opar. Her clever mind had invented a story that would satisfy the Oparians: a wonderful revelation from The Flaming God himself, ordering her to receive this stranger as a messenger to his worshippers. As for the man, she was sure he would prefer to be her husband rather than be sacrificed.

But when she had gone to tell him her plan, he seemed to have vanished, though the door remained tightly barred. Now he had returned out of thin air, and was killing her priests like sheep. For the moment she forgot her victim, and before she could gather her wits again the huge white man was standing before her. The intended sacrifice was in his arms, still in a faint.

"One side, La," he cried. "You saved me once, so I spare you; but do not interfere or attempt to follow, or I shall kill you also." As he spoke, he stepped past her toward the entrance to the vaults.

"Who is she?" asked the high priestess, pointing at Jane.

"She is mine," said Tarzan of the Apes.

For a moment La stared wide-eyed. Then her eyes filled with tears, a look of hopeless misery on her face. Right then a swarm of frightful men dashed past her to leap upon the ape-man, but Tarzan had already bounded into the passage leading to the pits below.

His pursuers followed cautiously, but when they found the chamber empty, they laughed and jabbered to each other. There being no other exit from the pits, they would watch and wait. But after awhile, they recalled that this same man had gotten out this way before, coming back again from the outside. They decided to send another fifty men out into the valley to recapture the man who had spoiled their ritual.

After Tarzan reached the well beyond the broken wall, he listened. Hearing no pursuit, he felt sure enough of his getaway that he took time to replace the tumbled stones. He did not want the Oparians to rediscover the way to the treasure chamber. One day he meant to return, and bear away an even greater fortune than he had already buried elsewhere.

On through the passageways he trotted, past the first door and through the treasure vault; past the second door and into the long, straight tunnel that led to the lofty hidden exit. Jane remained unconscious.

At the crest of the great boulder he halted to look back upon the city, and saw the hideous men

headed across the plain. Should he descend and make a race for the distant cliffs, or should he hide here until night? A glance at Jane's calm face made up his mind. He could not let their enemies get between them and freedom. They might have been followed through the tunnels as well. If they were surrounded, they would be captured, for he could not fight while carrying Jane.

To descend the steep face of the boulder carrying the woman was no easy task. By binding her across his shoulders with the grass rope, he succeeded in reaching the ground before the Oparians arrived. He descended on the far side from the city, so they would not be seen, and covered nearly a mile before the men of Opar rounded the granite sentinel and saw their quarry. With savage cries of delight, they broke into a mad run, expecting a quick capture.

With the athleticism of the ape-man and the short, crooked legs of the pursuers, Tarzan needed only to maintain an easy trot to keep them from gaining. Occasionally he would glance at the beautiful face, and feel her heartbeat to reassure himself she was alive.

Soon they reached the cliffs. During the last mile Tarzan had run full speed, so that he would have time to get down the cliffs before the Oparians could start throwing rocks down at them. He was half a mile down the mountainside before the fierce little men came panting up to the edge.

With cries of rage and disappointment they ranged along the cliff top shaking their clubs, but now they were discouraged. As Tarzan reached the woods that began at the base of the foothills, the men of Opar turned to go home.

Just within the forest, where he could yet watch the cliff tops, Tarzan laid Jane down on the grass. There was a stream nearby, and he brought water to bathe her face and hands, but she did not revive. Greatly worried, he gathered the girl into his strong arms once more and hurried on toward the west.

Late in the afternoon Jane Porter awoke. Was she dead? She recalled her final memories: the altar, the terrible priestess, the descending knife. Perhaps this was death, or maybe the knife was in her heart and this was some sort of before-death delirium.

When she finally worked up courage to open her eyes, what she saw confirmed her fears. She was being carried in the arms of her dead love, Tarzan, through a leafy paradise—Heaven! "If this be death," she murmured, "thank God that I am dead."

"You spoke, Jane!" cried Tarzan.

"Yes, Tarzan of the Apes," she replied, and for the first time in months a smile of peace and happiness lit up her face.

"Thank God!" cried the ape-man, stopping at a little grassy clearing beside a stream. "I was in time, after all."

"In time? What do you mean?" she questioned.

"In time to save you from death upon the altar, dear," he replied. "Do you not remember?"

"Save me from death?" she asked, in a puzzled tone. "Are we not both dead, my Tarzan?"

He set her down on the grass with her back resting against the trunk of a huge tree. "Dead!" he repeated, and then he laughed. "You are not dead, Jane, nor am I. My love, we are both very much alive."

"But both Hazel and Monsieur Thuran told me that you had fallen into the ocean many miles from land," she urged, as though trying to convince him that he must indeed be dead. "They said there was no chance you could have been rescued."

"I am no ghost," he said, with a laugh. "Yes,

the delightful Monsieur Thuran pushed me overboard, but I did not drown. I will tell you all about it after a while. I am the same wild man you first knew, Jane Porter."

The girl rose slowly to her feet and came toward him.

"I must be dreaming. I shall awaken in a moment to see that awful knife descending toward my heart—kiss me, dear, just once before I lose my dream forever."

Tarzan of the Apes needed no second invitation. He took the woman he loved in his strong arms, and kissed her not once, but a hundred times, until she lay there panting for breath; yet when he stopped she put her arms about his neck and drew his lips down to hers once more.

"Am I alive, or am I but a dream?" he asked.

"If you are not alive, my man," she answered, "this is a good way to die."

For a while, their gazes locked in silence as they luxuriated in the joy of the moment. It was Jane who broke it: "Where are we going, my love?" she asked. "What are we going to do?"

"Where would you like to go?" he asked. "What would you like to do?"

"To go where you go, my man; to do whatever seems best to you," she answered.

"But Clayton?" he asked. For a moment he had forgotten that anyone else existed. "We have forgotten your husband."

"I am not married, Tarzan, nor even engaged any more," she cried. "The day before those awful creatures captured me, I told Mr. Clayton of my love for you. He understood then that I could not keep my misguided promise. We had just been miraculously saved from a lion." She looked up at him in sudden realization. "Tarzan," she cried, "it was you!"

He dropped his eyes in shame.

"How could you have gone away and left me?" she cried reproachfully.

"Don't, Jane!" he pleaded. "I have suffered terrible guilt for that. You cannot imagine the jealous rage I felt. I was so bitter that I never again wanted to see a human being, so I went back to the apes." He told her everything since he had returned to the jungle. She asked him many questions, and at last fearfully raised the subject Monsieur Thuran had mentioned: the woman in Paris. He told her the story in full, for his heart had always been true to her. When he finished, he sat quietly awaiting her judgment.

"I knew that he was lying," she said. "Oh, what a horrible creature he is!"

"You are not angry with me, then?" he asked.

Her reply was completely irrelevant but truly feminine: "Is Olga de Coude very beautiful?"

And Tarzan laughed and kissed her again. "Not one-tenth as beautiful as you, dear," he said.

She gave a contented little sigh, and let her

head rest against his shoulder. He knew that he was forgiven.

That night Tarzan built a snug little platform high among the swaying branches of a giant tree. There she slept, while in a fork beneath her the ape-man kept guard and rested, ready to protect her.

It took them many happy days to reach the coast. Where possible, they walked hand in hand; when the brush was thick, he carried her lightly through the trees. If it were not for their urgency to help Clayton, they would have made the wonderful journey last even longer.

On the last day before they reached the coast Tarzan scented men ahead of them. He cautioned Jane to silence. "There are few friends in the jungle," he remarked dryly.

In half an hour they came quietly up on a small party of African warriors marching west. Tarzan gave a cry of delight—it was a band of his own Waziri, including Busuli and other veterans of Opar. At the sight of him they danced for joy. They had been searching for him for weeks, they explained.

The Waziri were quite curious about Jane, and when they found that she was to be his mate, they treated her with great honor. With the happy Waziri laughing and dancing around them they reached the primitive shelter by the shore.

There was no sign of life, and no response to their calls. Tarzan clambered quickly up to the little tree hut, only to emerge a moment later with an empty tin. Throwing it down to Busuli, he asked him to fetch water, and then he beckoned Jane to come up.

Together they leaned over the starved thing that once had been an English nobleman. Tears came to Jane's eyes as she saw the poor, sunken cheeks and hollow eyes in that once young and handsome face.

"He still lives," said Tarzan. "We will do all we can, but I fear that we are too late."

When Busuli had brought the water Tarzan forced a few drops between Clayton's cracked and swollen lips. He wiped the hot forehead and bathed the pitiful limbs.

Presently Clayton opened his eyes. A faint, shadowy smile lit his face as he saw the girl leaning over him. At sight of Tarzan, the expression changed to wonder.

"It's all right, old fellow," said the ape-man. "We've found you in time. We'll have you on your feet again before you know it."

The Englishman shook his head weakly. "It's too late," he whispered. "But it's just as well. I'd rather die."

"Where is Monsieur Thuran?" asked the girl.

"He is a devil! He took off after my fever got really bad. When I was too weak to fetch my own water . . . I begged him to get some for me . . . when he returned, he drank it in front of me and threw the rest on the floor . . . he laughed in my face!"

At the thought of it, Clayton gained a bit of strength, and raised himself upon one elbow. "Yes," he almost shouted; "I will live. I will live long enough to find and kill that beast!" But the brief effort weakened him, and he sank back again.

"Don't worry about Thuran," said Tarzan, laying a reassuring hand on Clayton's forehead. "I shall get him in the end, never fear."

For a long time Clayton lay very still. Several times Tarzan had to put his ear quite close to the sunken chest to catch his faint heartbeat. Toward evening he stirred again for a brief moment.

"Jane," he whispered. She bent her head closer to hear. "I have wronged you—and him," he nodded weakly toward the ape-man. "It is no excuse, but I loved you too much to think of giving you up. I do not ask your forgiveness. I only wish to do now what I should have done over a year ago." He fumbled in the pocket of the overcoat beneath him, drawing forth a crumpled bit of yellow paper. He handed it to the girl, and with that his arm fell limply across his chest, his head dropped back, and, with a little gasp, he was still. Tarzan of the Apes slowly drew a fold of the coat across the upturned face of his one-time rival.

For a moment they knelt there, the girl's lips moving in silent prayer. As they rose and stood on either side of the peaceful form, tears came to the ape-man's eyes, for in the anguish of his own heart, he had learned compassion for the suffering of others.

Through her own tears the girl read the message on the paper, and her eyes went very wide. Twice she read those startling words before she fully understood.

Fingerprints prove you Greystoke.
      Congratulations.
      D'ARNOT

She handed the paper to Tarzan. "And he has known it all this time," she said, "and did not tell you?"

"I knew it first, Jane," he replied. "I did not know that he had any idea. I must have dropped this message that night in the waiting room, just after I received it."

"And afterward you told us that your mother was a she-ape, and that you had never known your father?" she asked incredulously.

"The title and the estates meant nothing to me without you, my dear," he replied. "And if I had taken them away from him I would have taken them from the woman I love—don't you understand, Jane?"

She extended her arms toward him across the body of the dead man, and took his hands in hers.

"And I would have thrown away a love like that!" she said.

CHAPTER 26

The Passing of the Ape-Man

The next morning they made the short journey to Tarzan's cabin, with four proud Waziri warriors carrying the Englishman to his final rest. The ape-man had suggested that Clayton be buried beside the former Lord Greystoke near the latter's cabin. Jane Porter approved of both the plan and Tarzan's tender-hearted chivalry—the sign of a civilized man.

They were halfway there when the lead Waziri scouts stopped suddenly, pointing in amazement at a strange figure approaching them along the beach. It was a man with a shiny silk hat, walking slowly with bent head and hands clasped behind him. He wore a long, black frock coat.

Jane Porter cried out in joy and ran quickly ahead. The old man looked up, and soon he too cried out in relief and happiness. As Professor Archimedes Q. Porter folded his daughter in his arms tears streamed down his elderly face, and it was several minutes before he could speak.

When he recognized Tarzan, they had a hard time convincing the Professor that he could believe his eyes. Like the other members of the party, he had been certain that the ape-man was dead. The old man was deeply touched at the news of Clayton's death.

"I cannot understand it," said the Professor. "Monsieur Thuran assured us that Clayton passed away many days ago."

"Thuran is with you?" asked Tarzan.

"Yes; he recently found us. We were camped just a short distance north of your cabin. Bless me, but he will be delighted to see you both."

"And surprised," commented Tarzan.

A short time later the strange party came to the ape-man's cabin. The clearing was filled with people coming and going, and almost the first one Tarzan saw was D'Arnot.

"Paul!" cried the ape-man. "In the name of sanity what are you doing here? Or are we all insane?"

D'Arnot's presence was quickly explained, however, as were many other strange things. D'Arnot's ship had been patrolling the coast, when, at the lieutenant's suggestion, they had anchored off the little harbor for another look at the cabin and the jungle in which many of the ship's company had ventured two years before. Ashore they had found Lord Tennington's party, and were preparing to carry them all back to civilization.

Esmeralda, Hazel Strong, her mother, and Mr. Samuel T. Philander were delighted by Jane

Porter's safe return. Her escape seemed too miraculous for anyone but Tarzan of the Apes to have managed. They showered the uncomfortable ape-man with praise and attention until he wished he were back in the amphitheater of the apes.

Among the Waziri and the Americans and French there was much interest, and Tarzan translated as they shared their stories. What each side could not say with language was said with the universal language of friendly eyes and polite respect. When the tales were told, Busuli came forth to clasp D'Arnot's hand, as one leader of warriors, and friend of Tarzan, to another. The Frenchman's eyes mingled pleasure and regret as he remembered what had been done to another tribe for his sake, and he took the African's hand in his own.

They all exchanged gifts, but the Africans were saddened to realize that their king would soon be sailing away from them on the great canoe far out from shore.

As yet, the newcomers had seen nothing of Lord Tennington and Monsieur Thuran. They had gone out hunting early in the day, and had not yet returned.

"This evil man, whose name you say is Rokoff, will be very surprised to see you," Jane said to Tarzan.

"His surprise will be short-lived," replied the ape-man grimly, and something in his tone made her look up into his face in alarm. What she saw confirmed her fears. She pleaded with him to leave the Russian to the laws of France: "In the heart of the jungle, dear," she said, "with no other form of justice but your own mighty muscles, you would be justified in sentencing this man to the fate he deserves. Here, with a civilized government at hand, it would be murder.

"There would be a terrible confrontation. Your friends would have to watch you arrested," she continued, "or you might have to flee once again into your jungle. We would all be miserable, especially me, for I cannot bear to lose you again. Promise me that you will only turn him over to Captain Dufranne, and let the law take its course. This beast is not worth risking our happiness for."

Tarzan saw the wisdom of her appeal, and promised. He went to explain the matter to the French captain, who agreed to see justice done.

A half hour later 'Thuran' and Tennington emerged from the jungle side by side. Tennington was the first to note strangers in the camp. He saw the black warriors talking in dialect with the sailors from the cruiser, and then he saw a lithe, brown giant talking with Lieutenant D'Arnot and Captain Dufranne.

"Who is that, I wonder," said Tennington to Rokoff, and as the Russian raised his eyes and met those of the ape-man, he staggered and went white.

"Saints!" he cried, and before Tennington realized what was happening, Rokoff had his rifle leveled at Tarzan. He pulled the trigger, but the Englishman was close enough to deflect the barrel just before the hammer fell. The bullet intended for Tarzan's heart whirred harmlessly above his head.

Before the Russian could fire again, the apeman was upon him and had wrestled the firearm away. Captain Dufranne, Lieutenant D'Arnot, and a dozen sailors had rushed up at the sound of the shot, and now Tarzan turned the Russian over to them without a word.

The cold eyes of the Waziri made their desires clear, but Tarzan spoke to them, explaining that the assassin would likely spend many years in a cage with other human beasts for his crimes. At this they relented, but Rokoff shuddered at the sight of many sets of angry eyes burning his image into their brains, sentencing him to death should he ever again set foot in their portion of Africa.

The captain gave immediate orders to place the Russian in irons and confine him on board the cruiser. Just before the guard escorted the prisoner into the small boat, Tarzan asked permission to search him. To his delight, he found the stolen papers.

The shot had brought Jane Porter and the others from the cabin, and a moment after the excitement had died down she greeted the surprised Lord Tennington. Tarzan joined them after he had taken the papers from Rokoff, and, as he approached, Jane Porter introduced him to Tennington.

"Lord Tennington, I want you to meet Tarzan of the Apes, soon to be known as Lord Greystoke," she said.

The Englishman's astonishment overcame his best efforts at courtesy, and the strange story of the ape-man had to be told to him many times by Tarzan, Jane Porter and Lieutenant D'Arnot to convince Lord Tennington that they were not all quite insane.

At sunset they buried William Cecil Clayton beside the jungle graves of his uncle and his aunt, the former Lord and Lady Greystoke. At Tarzan's request, French rifles fired three volleys over the last resting place of "a brave man, who met his death with honor."

Professor Porter, who in his younger days had been ordained a minister, conducted the simple services for the dead. Around the grave, with bowed heads, stood as strange a company of mourners as ever attended a funeral. There were French officers and sailors in full dress, two English lords, Americans, and a score of proud African warriors.

Following the funeral Tarzan asked Captain Dufranne to delay sailing for a couple of days while he went inland a few miles to fetch his "belongings," and the officer gladly granted the favor. Tarzan, king of the Waziri, summoned his warriors and vanished into the jungle.

Late the next afternoon they returned with the first load of "belongings," and when the party saw the ancient ingots of virgin gold they had a thousand questions; but he offered no clue as to the source of his immense treasure. "I left a thousand behind," he explained, "for every one that I brought away, and when these are spent I may wish to return for more."

The next day he returned to camp with the rest of his ingots, and, when they were stored on board, Captain Dufranne said he felt like the commander of an old-time Spanish galleon returning from the Aztec treasure cities. "I hope my crew will not cut my throat, and take over the ship," he added jokingly.

The next morning, as they were preparing to embark, Tarzan made a suggestion to Jane Porter.

"Wild beasts are not supposed to be sentimental," he said, "but nevertheless I would like to be married in the cabin where I was born, beside the graves of my mother and my father, and surrounded by the savage jungle that always has been my home."

"I know of no other place where I would rather be married to my forest god than beneath the shade of his forest," concurred Jane. "Let us ask the others."

Their friends assured them that it was a perfect way to celebrate their remarkable romance. So the entire party assembled within the little cabin and just outside the door to witness Professor Porter's second ministerial duty in a span of three days. D'Arnot was to be best man, and Hazel Strong bridesmaid, when Tennington upset all the arrangements with another of his marvelous "ideas."

"If Mrs. Strong is agreeable," he said, taking the bridesmaid's hand in his, "Hazel and I think it would be ripping to make it a double wedding." And it was—though perhaps the strangest wedding and feast any of them would ever experience.

The next day they sailed. As the cruiser steamed slowly out to sea, Mr. and Mrs. John Clayton—now Lord and Lady Greystoke—leaned against the rail to watch the shoreline fade. There danced twenty Waziri warriors, waving their spears above their heads, and shouting farewells to their departing king.

"I would hate to think that I am looking upon the jungle for the last time, my dear," he said, "except that I know that I am going to a new world of happiness with you forever."

And with that, Tarzan of the Apes bent down and kissed his mate.

AFTERWORD

About the Author

Everyone has heard of Tarzan, but few know much about his creator, one of the great pioneers of modern fiction: Edgar Rice Burroughs.

This adventure author's amazingly productive life can be divided neatly into halves: To use some images from *Tarzan*, Edgar Rice Burrough's first thirty-seven years were spent banging into one tree after another. But he spent his remaining thirty-eight years swinging through them with all the grace of his most famous literary creation.

Ed, as his family called him, was born into the comfortable middle-class family of George and Mary Evaline Burroughs in Chicago, Illinois on February 23, 1875, the youngest of four boys. George and Mary Evaline had married while George was a Union officer during the Civil War, and they were now highly respectable pillars of Chicago society. Ed's later actions would show his parents to be very patient and loving people.

Ed was a likable boy with a happy enough child-hood. He was a bit of a troublemaker, but the constant flow of diseases through the school system in those days did far more harm to Ed's education than his inability to behave. In the late 1800s the flu was much deadlier than it is today, and Ed got sick often. Mr. and Mrs. Burroughs feared for their son's life in the crowded, polluted city, so when he was sixteen, they sent him packing to the brand-new state of Idaho to live a healthier life in the clean air of his uncle's cattle ranch.

It was a loving move, but a naïve one that they would soon regret. The adventuresome teen loved the rough-and-ready life of Idaho. The cowboys of 1891 were often gamblers, outlaws in hiding, or worse; and Ed had a fine time listening to their tall tales. Basically, Ed was a sixteen-year-old boy learning from men how to get into man-sized trouble. His uncle did not protest, but his parents were another matter. Hanging around with shady characters and learning bad habits was not what they had in mind for their son, and they hurried him back to the Midwest.

Mr. and Mrs. Burroughs then tried sending their son to two different boarding schools, and the reports on his wild behavior only increased their worries. In those days, wealthy people with bad-boy sons often sent their sons away to private military schools for straightening out. Accordingly, in early 1892 Ed was packed off to the Michigan Military Academy for his high school education. That wasn't any help either. While Ed liked the idea of military life, it had too many rules and regulations, many of which he broke. As a cadet, he rose in rank only to find himself in trouble again. He was good at football and popular with his peers, but that did not help his grades and his behavior, which ranged from mediocre to bad. Only his father's influence enabled Ed to graduate.

After graduation, Ed taught briefly at the academy. It hardly suited his taste for adventure, and he soon joined the United States Cavalry. He was sent to the then-Arizona Territory in 1896 and discovered that peacetime Army life was mostly about manual labor. He hoped to become an officer, but his tendency toward poor health dictated otherwise, and he was discharged in 1897.

For the next three years, Ed went from art school in Chicago to his uncle's ranch to running a small business in Idaho. Then, in 1900, after ten years of turning down his proposals, his childhood sweetheart Emma Hurlbert agreed to marry him; they eventually had two sons and a daughter together. For the next twelve years, the future giant of fiction and his family barely managed to scrape by. At one point, they had to pawn Emma's jewelry to buy food. Ed bounced from job to job during that time, from office manager to railroad policeman to salesman, and he even applied without success to become an officer in the Chinese Army. While borrowing money to pay rent and feed his family, Ed could not have imagined what a different future awaited him.

In 1910, Ed made a cynical but practical decision. Having read a lot of 'pulp fiction'—typically romances, westerns, and other action-packed writing not generally considered literature—he decided he could write similar stories. In 1911, Edgar Rice

Burroughs sold his first written work, introducing John Carter as the hero of *Under the Moons of Mars*. This led to a series of adventures now considered science fiction classics. Burroughs had finally found his calling.

Shortly thereafter, in 1912, Burroughs sold *Tarzan of the Apes* to a magazine for $700. It was published in book form in 1914 and soon sold over a million copies—a remarkable number for the times. Burroughs went on to write a total of twenty-six books about the ape-man. They succeeded beyond his wildest expectations, and they capture readers' imagination to this day.

We can probably thank Hollywood for some of Tarzan's popularity. Not everyone knew how to read a book, but almost anyone could go to a movie, even if they could not read the subtitles. In 1918, when movies were still silent, the first *Tarzan* film was produced. When the Olympic swimming hero Johnny Weissmuller began to play the ape-man in 1932, and sound was added to movies, Tarzan became what Luke Skywalker or Indiana Jones would later become: not merely a hero, but a household name.

No one seemed more surprised by his success than Burroughs himself. He was a refreshingly candid man who disliked bragging. In his own words: "I have been successful probably because I have always realized that I knew nothing about writing and have merely tried to tell an interesting story entertainingly."

Burroughs's later life included a divorce and remarriage, a stint as a town mayor, and the purchase of a California ranch called "Tarzana," which in 1928 became the name of a town that thrives to this day. Burroughs was playing tennis with his son in Hawaii on December 7, 1941, when the smoke began to rise from the bombing of Pearl Harbor by Japan. At 66, he was too old to enlist in the Army, but not too old for adventure; he went to work as a war correspondent, and even flew along on bombing missions with the Army Air Corps.

Edgar Rice Burroughs passed away in 1950 of a heart ailment; fittingly, he was reading a comic book in bed at the time.

His greatest adventure hero, Tarzan of the Apes, lives on, probably for generations yet to come.

About *The Return of Tarzan*

When *Tarzan of the Apes* came out in 1912, it made a terrific splash in the world of 'pulp fiction'—that is, novels written purely for entertainment. Readers shouted for more, and they got their wish the very next year when Edgar Rice Burroughs published *The Return of Tarzan*. This 1913 sequel was met with equal enthusiasm. Now here we are, nearly a century later, still enjoying the adventures of the hero who is both Lord Greystoke and jungle king.

The continued popularity of the Tarzan books isn't something to be taken for granted. Consider the titles of a few other best-selling novels of 1913: *The Valiants of Virginia, The Judgment House,*

Heart of the Hills. You've never heard of them? Don't feel bad; most people today haven't. It's unlikely that any of them are still in print. They've faded from public view, as most fiction does a few years after it's published.

But Tarzan lives on. Burroughs' books have never gone out of print, and the character of Tarzan has become firmly embedded in modern culture. We not only have Burroughs' 26 volumes of Tarzan stories (including such titles as *Tarzan and the Lost Empire*, *Tarzan at the Earth's Core*, and *Tarzan and the Leopard Men*); but we have spin-offs of every imaginable kind. The movie versions began appearing in 1918, and they're still coming. Highlights include a tremendously popular series of films in the 1930s and '40s, starring Olympic swimming champion Johnny Weissmuller. More recent Tarzan films have been 1984's *Greystoke: The Legend of Tarzan,* and the 1999 animated Disney version. There has been a Tarzan TV series; Tarzan action figures and lunch boxes; Tarzan video games, and even a funny Tarzan-inspired cartoon series and movie, *George of the Jungle.* And who among us doesn't recognize the Tarzan yell when we hear it? (Give credit to actor Weissmuller for that one.)

So why hasn't Tarzan gone the route of the other 1913 best-sellers and faded into oblivion? Clearly, in creating the Tarzan series, author Burroughs tapped into something with boundless ability to interest readers. And what is that something? It's not merely the appeal of a great adventure story—although heaven knows Burroughs is a master at coming up with exciting plots that are full of action, double-crossing, cowardice, and heroism. It's not just that people love exotic locales—although they do, and, again, Burroughs knows how to drop his readers into the rain forests of Africa or a café full of suspicious characters in an Algerian back alley. No, it's something more fundamental than that. It's his central character: Tarzan, Lord Greystoke. What a stroke of genius Burroughs had when he came up with Tarzan! Whether he realized it or not (and chances are he did), he was appealing to two very basic human stories—so basic, you might even call them myths.

One of the stories that Tarzan grew out of is as old as the book of Genesis. It tells of a man, a physically perfect human being, who lives in the garden of Eden. Doesn't Tarzan remind you of the Bible's first man, Adam, as he grows to adulthood in the African forest? Like Adam, he lives in a paradise where he only has to reach out his hand to find delicious fruit, ripe for the taking. Like Adam, he is master of the animals around him, and they recognize his kingship. And most fundamentally: like Adam, Tarzan grows lonely. He wants another of his own kind, although he does not understand his own loneliness until he is confronted with Jane, a lovely woman. Once he gets a glimpse of Jane and her world, he realizes that he must leave his innocent Eden.

Another timeless myth that the Tarzan story

taps into of is what we might call the Cinderella story. We're all familiar with Cinderella, the poor, unwanted child, abused by her stepmother and selfish stepsisters, who is swept away from her humble beginning to live as a princess. The theme of Cinderella is one that is nearly as old as humanity itself. Who among us hasn't dreamed, if only briefly, that we don't belong to our own, ordinary family? Haven't you imagined, just for a moment, that you really belong to a family of royalty—or wild dancing gypsies—or circus performers—or at least that you're the long-lost grandchild of a lonely old millionaire? (If you've read any of the *Harry Potter* books, you'll recognize that these massively popular works also play upon this theme, as poor unwanted Harry is finally recognized as the son of wizard nobility.) By making Tarzan not only a perfect, natural he-man but also the rich and noble Lord Greystoke, Burroughs satisfies our desire to have all our fairy tales come true. We have the fun of seeing our hero swing through the trees of Eden, living the natural life of a primitive animal, all the time knowing that he has a fortune and title awaiting him in England.

As we identify with Burroughs' creation, Tarzan the Ape-Man, we satisfy several of our most deeply-held desires. This satisfaction has insured our pleasure in reading the Tarzan stories for many years. Chances are that our enjoyment of these stories will endure for many more!